The Young Garden Manifesto

Cameron Lambright

-INCANDESCENCE PRESS-

INCANDESCENCE PRESS
www.incandescencepress.com

For Erica, who wrestled demons off my shoulders.

Every story that was ever told, in the whole history of the world, is a story about a young man and a young woman. You might not believe that, but it's probably true. My story was no different than yours. It was profoundly more the same.

Then, why didn't it feel that way?

CHAPTER 1

A YOUNG MAN GREW up in the village of York. He was talented and handsome, he won at all the games. He was kind, too, and gentle. He was sublime too, and genteel. In the village of York. His name was Adam, and he was their treasured son.

York was an ancient village. It had ancient people of ancient ways. Nothing there had ever changed, for uncounted years. Though they had their stories. Wars and rumours of wars. Long ago. Whispers heard from afar. Stories to tell them who they were and who they are. For thousands of thousands of years.

That is, for as long as anyone could imagine.

It was made entirely of stone. York was. Hard stone, not like we have. Enduring, like builded diamonds. Little stone buildings and big stone buildings, round buildings and square. Buildings that rose to the roof of the sky, and buildings dug deep to the depths of the earth itself. York was a grand city; nevertheless, it was a village.

cut

Blood pooled in Adam's wounds and ran to the ground. His throat felt like paper, he couldn't swallow. He tried to raise his arm, but it seemed apart from him. An indifferent object in the dirt. For some reason he didn't hurt. A patch of darkness drifted across the starry night sky.

"Is this the way it ends?"

Raindrops poured into his open mouth. They tasted like

iron. And like God. They lubricated his coagulating chest.

He was too young to regret dying. It inspired no emotion, only surprise.

"It seems stupid to die," Adam thought.

The rain passed on across the sky. As Adam's eyes closed, he could taste moonlight on his tongue. Later, he hurt again, and knew that he would live. It seemed funny.

cut

Every building that had ever been had always been, for as long as anyone could remember. And every building and every road, and every table and every tool, were made of stone. The gardens themselves were stone, in York. Some garden stones had moss. And the rivers and streams that ran through the town. The ground was stone.

York had strong, high, thick walls, surrounded on every side by tilled fields and apple groves. Beyond them lay the forest. Wild wilderness and gardens. Rich, dark earth nourished by pure waters. Huge trees — fruit and oak and evergreen — sweet flowers, mosses, grass on verdant hills. Some weeds, of course, some thistles and nettles. Some hornets and some vipers. Full, wild land, as far as the eye could see. And the gardens, too. Some here, some there, some far away.

Perhaps it was curious that they chose to live in stone. The people of York. They didn't know why they did. Only, it was the way they had always lived, since long ago. In their fine stone city. Or village, if you like. No one ever thought to change.

When a boy was ready to become a man, he entered the tending age. It meant he must go into the wilderness and make a garden of his own. A real garden, of vegetables and fruits, not like the stone gardens in the village. He must find and cultivate the garden himself, and bring its harvest back to York. Then he could take a wife. These were the laws in that land.

Some young men, if their gardens were very close, could live in the village, and work in their gardens during the day. Others tended farther off, but could still come home when they wished. Some worked deep within the forest, and returned to York only after their crop came in. At the season end they each brought their yield, some ten fold, some one hundred fold, some fifty. Each according to his abilities. The garden itself played no small role in its fruit.

Adam visited his grandfather before the tending day.

"Grandfather," Adam said, "in three days I will leave York. I have been well educated in the art of tending. In the tilling and the seeding, irrigation and fertilization, in guarding and weeding, the waiting, and the harvesting. I am young and stron-"

"And yet," his Grandfather interrupted him.

"I have decided that I will make a garden deep within the forest. Tell me your advice."

His grandfather looked up and down at him. At the life playing out before his eyes. He appraised it. Stared.

cut

The fish were silver, long and thin. They rose out of the lake like needles from the surface of a mirror. Cartwheeling into the air, and splashing back. He had never seen anything like them. He was starving, if not unhappily, and they looked good to eat. That would take more time than he could spare. Adam lay down in the mud and stared out across the sky reflected water, resting.

Her voice echoed over him here. Not the words, the sound of it. Like music. And he made up his own words to fit the tune, and they seemed right, and he smiled. Then he was in pain again.

He pushed upright against the bark of a tree, and walked back into the forest.

cut

"What did they tell you in school, to start a new garden or to find an abandoned garden and continue the work from there?"

"To find an abandoned garden, of course," Adam said quickly. "Only a fool would start a new garden, when work can be saved using one already made. I know the location of an old garden: huge, flat, with good earth. More than one, in fact."

"Only a fool? Is that what they taught you. So you never thought to start a garden of your own, from scratch?"

"Do you say that I should?"

Adam's grandfather got up from the table and walked to the hearth in the front room. He picked up a long stone implement and stirred the burning wood. After a few minutes standing, he rested his limbs on the stone rocking chair that sat by the hearth.

"Come, Adam, sit with me by the fire."

Adam bowed his head modestly and sat in the other chair beside the flames. It was lower than the rocking chair, stool-like, a little closer to the fire, but finely crafted.

"Think of how long our people have been doing everything the same way. The same. Always the same. Day in, day out, year in year out, life in life out, nothing ever to change, or-"

"But that's what makes York perfect," Adam interrupted. "I have heard the legends of other cities, the cities from ages ago. That they rebuilt their houses all the time, and were always becoming different. That they destroyed themselves. We were taught of a land where the people sing a new song every year at harvest time, and the old songs are all forgotten. But we sing the same song every year, so that everyone knows it and loves it, and it is never forgotten. Grandfather, we were told of a land where men and women would be born and grow up, and never even find their place in their own city! They didn't even know what they were supposed to be. It's so terrible."

"Adam," his Grandfather said the name sympathetically. "Do you know what 'stagnation' means?"

"No."

" 'Stagnation' is an ancient word. Few of us know it anymore," the old voice trailed off wistfully into nothing.

Adam's grandfather cleared his throat and resumed, "To speak it in the village square could be blasphemy. It means that something is no longer improving, that things have stopped getting better. It means that everything is simply staying the same. We, York, have known stagnation for a very long time."

"But-"

"Listen to me. I am an old man. I have seen many things. I have heard many tales. And I have heard the stories that are not told. Stories of York before the ancient histories. When things changed. When our people were learning, and improving; real learning, where knowledge builds on knowledge that builds on knowledge and it reaches to the sky! Look at us today, boy, could you and your friends or could your father build the city that you live in? No. But your father's fathers' fathers built it!

"You have come to me for advice, so let me give you my advice. It is the wisdom of an old man; bear it as you may. When you go to find your garden, find a new, virginal garden to cultivate. Don't follow exactly what you have been told. Try different things, Adam. Things that occur to you."

"But, Grandfather–"

"That is my advice, Adam. Bear it as you will. My grandfather gave me the same advice when I was your age, and I could not. That was many years ago. But *you* can do it, boy. You can!"

"Grandfather, I will think on it."

"Good, think. Thinking is the pastime of the gods. Or, some would say: God."

Before sunrise, as his father fussed over the collection of tools and equipment for his journey, Adam caught a few happy, private moments with his mother. She was laughing, reminiscing over tales of his childhood, of who he was before he could remember who he was. Adam changed the subject abruptly.

"Mother," he said, "before I go, tell me one last bit of advice, some wisdom or secret that will help me with the tending."

"Goodness, Adam," his mother said, with a pleased embarrassment, "you know everything you need to know about the tending already. You're more prepared than any young man I have ever seen. I'm sure you will return with a wonderful crop."

"No," Adam insisted, "that's not enough, there must be something more."

"Child. Our knowledge in this life is not perfect. We can only understand a thing so well, then all that is left is to do it, to try, and to hope it comes together. It usually does. Somehow it just does."

Adam frowned at the earth. His mother smiled, remembering the same expression from his infancy, barely suppressing a laugh.

"Well, honey," she rejoined the subject, "if there is one thing I can tell you, it's just to be careful out there and come home safe. The men make light of it, but there are dangers in the forest. Be safe, that is your mother's advice."

It was sound advice, but he paid it only passing heed.

Adam left that morning before sunrise, carrying two heavy packs upon his shoulders as well as his stone farming tools. A burdensome load. He left his parents at the family doorstep, and walked by himself toward the quiet city gates. This was the way he wanted it: the beginning of the journey, his journey, without further ado.

As he walked through the city, he was greeted by a powerful man in York, an old friend of his father's.

"Ho, Adam! Well met, son, well met! Today is the day, is it?"

"Today is the day, sir," Adam said politely, as the older man fell into his stride.

"And are you well prepared for the journey at hand?" the gentleman wondered jovially.

"Well," Adam began to reply.

"Of course you are!" the man boomed. "I know that. I know it as well as anybody. Everyone in York is very proud of you Adam, you are our golden child."

"Thank you," Adam said, without slowing in his march to the gates.

"Well that's just why I wanted to talk to you this morning, Adam. You are destined to have a brilliant tending, and why shouldn't you, hmm? Why shouldn't you indeed. You see, I have in my hands a map to the most lush, perfect, pristine garden plot in the entire forest. The most. No, don't say it, I'll tell you: it has lain fallow for decades. Decades! I have been waiting and waiting for the right young man to come along, who deserves to know the location of this garden, who absolutely must know. Adam, you're the one."

cut

Adam pulled her body against him. She smelled so clean. She giggled and pretended to push away, but squeezed up tighter. He touched her. He touched her everywhere. He didn't know why he did. Only, because he wanted to, and because she liked it. He rubbed his body against her, and she laughed and rubbed back, and rolled over him, and he touched her more, and their skin pressed together until they couldn't remember anything else, feeling anything else, until they felt like the same person.

And they couldn't breathe, and it was good.

"Isn't this a better place to sleep," Adam said, as their dreams began to overcome them, "than out there."

cut

The gentleman pressed a folded parchment furtively into Adam's hand. Adam looked curiously at it.

"No, no, of course you don't have to use it. I wouldn't hold it against you. Maybe you already have your plot of land picked out. Maybe you are thinking to overtake the same land your father once worked. *Maybe* you are thinking to make a new garden of your own. Some have. But the map is yours, boy, do with it what you wish. It was my garden, Adam, many, many years ago. It was the thing that launched me on my way. What earth! What earth."

"Thank you, sir," Adam said sincerely, stuffing the map into a pocket. "I have not yet decided what course I will take, but I am grateful for your generosity, and your faith in me."

"Not at all, not at all. However you proceed, I'm sure that you will be mightily successful. Mightily. I would wish you luck, but you will not need it."

"Godspeed, my boy," the gentleman concluded, slapping Adam on the back, "and congratulations!"

Adam crossed the threshold of the city. Early rising farmers already preceded him, preparing great city tracts for planting in the coming weeks. He called greetings to them as he passed, but never paused in his inexorable march to the forest. He was eager to leave York and its denizens behind, in his rush to become a man. To venture into the wild on his own, at last. And live life, he thought. Put pen to parchment of the universe and write his story. He could not begin it soon enough. Shade from the tall, steady, phalanx of trees enveloped him.

violin and cello w/ brass band. allegro.

Bear with me here....

OUR PLANE TOUCHED down on schedule, August 14, at 4:25 p.m. The flight from Denver had been uneventful, although the old Boeing jet shook frighteningly during takeoff and landing. La Guardia Airport's runways begin right up against the water's edge, so as you land it seems as if you're crashing into the bay. I was traveling to New York from Eugene, Oregon. Moving away from home for the first time. That would have been excitement enough.

The passengers on the plane were an odd mix. Two gay men had almost gotten into a fight over the overhead storage space. Fists had been threatened, but not thrown. F-words had been exchanged. They were both with their apparent partners, both middle-aged, but while one was covered in tattoos and piercings, and accompanied by a very tall shemale, the other was dressed like a retired grandfather and accompanied by a fellow of similar deportment. That's a funny kind of culture clash, I guess. 50% or more of the passengers on the flight from Denver were gay, overreaching even the New York City stereotype by a wide margin, so you could say that New York's gay community was well represented. But not by those two.

Sitting in front of me was a boisterous contingent of professional skateboarders. I occupied a window seat beside two octogenarians, and, although one of them struggled vainly against the mechanism of her seat belt, refusing to allow it to be explained, they were pleasant enough. Young, and a bit sheltered, this was my first time traveling anywhere alone. I felt more anxious than boisterous.

We waited on the runway to begin exiting the plane. Most of the passengers squeezed themselves into the center aisle when our pilot informed us that power was out at the airport and we would have to exit through the rear on a portable stairway. The wait for the stairway would be "about 15 minutes".

After at least 20 minutes had passed, the pilot informed us that there were only two mobile stairways in the entire airport, so we would have to wait a while longer before they could borrow one from another airline. This was fine for most of us, but the frail old women next to me were not fit for climbing stairs. One of them had been expecting wheel-chair service. They waited out the next half hour nervously, steeling themselves for the task ahead. The portable stair-way arrived, and it was their only available option.

The ladies were stoic about it, though. Their patient attitude made it easier for me not to be irritated about the delay. I do get a bit claustrophobic in cramped up places with no proper exits, like planes. The woman needing a wheelchair insisted that she could climb the stairs just fine as long as someone would hold her cane while she gripped the rails with both hands. I held her cane and went first, trying to make sure neither of them fell as we went down the stairs. No problem. At the bottom, I handed the woman her cane back, smiled, watched her sit down in a waiting wheelchair, smiled again, and walked quickly away. It felt good to be out in the open. Better than good.

"Thank goodness that ordeal is over," I thought to myself, sucking in great gulps of fresh air to match my long strides across the tarmac.

Inside, the airport was chaotic. The bathrooms, thank goodness, were dimly lit with generator power, although their toilets did not appear to be flushing anymore. I guess their automatic mechanisms needed electricity.

As we all walked to collect our bags, we kept asking

each other about the power outage. When would the power be back? What had happened? A respectable looking family man said there was a blackout reaching all the way to Detroit. That seemed unlikely. Everyone crossed their fingers hoping the power would be back soon, assuming it would be, and hoping, in any event, that this power outage had not been caused by terrorist attack.

Our bags were brought out manually by the airline's baggage workers, although one of the non-budget companies had a baggage conveyor belt that was still running. After standing at the baggage carousel for at least 45 minutes, I finally got my bags. Thank God. Now to get out of here! I assumed the power would come back any minute. At home, in Oregon, we had never had a power outage that lasted longer than an hour or two. And this was New York City, after all.

I wheeled my bags up to the shuttle and taxi counter. *Maybe there are still some shuttles running.* The attendant there sort of smirked at me when I asked.

"Only Taxis," he said blankly, in a thick, miscellaneous accent.

Very helpful.

I rolled my bags outside, or at least I rolled one (the other three I had to carry), and observed the line to catch a Yellow Cab. There were about 50 people in line already.

"This is the line for a taxi?"

I might as well make sure.

"It starts back there!"

They point their fingers so impatiently. Sigh.

I stood in line. I figured I was in a little over my head, since I'd only ridden a cab once before in my life and didn't know a soul in New York. The power outage was not my biggest concern, I assumed it would be over soon enough. Which is not to say that I wasn't talking to the people around me about it; it was our chief source of conversation. I asked the girl in front of me where she was heading to.

"Manhattan."

Katie, that was her name, wasn't as blank as the sentence looks, though. Actually, she was pretty friendly, and we struck up a conversation. Katie was familiar with the law school that I had come to New York to attend; she had done her undergraduate work nearby and had an ex-boyfriend who had gone there. She was working as a first grade teacher in Queens and finishing up a Master's degree at Queens College.

"You can catch a cab with me if you want," she said.

"Sure," I accepted quickly, "that would be great! I really don't know what I'm doing anyway."

Immediately, an illicit cab driver walked by offering to take someone to Manhattan.

"How much?" we ask.

"$35... each."

Katie thought the price was outrageous, which it probably was.

"I trust the Yellow Cabs," she said. "It's not worth taking a chance when the price isn't even halfway decent."

It seemed so true.

Eventually, we made it to the front of the line and a cab pulled up.

"Where?" the cabby asked, in an Indian accent. "Manhattan? No, it's too far, I don't have enough gas."

When we did not immediately throw our bags into the

trunk, the supervisor came over to see what our problem was.

"Get in, what are you guys waiting for?"

"He says he doesn't have enough gas."

The supervisor leaned in to look at the fuel gauge in the cab.

"He has enough. Better take the cab while you still can."

Our driver looked uncertain, but bowed before the authority opinion. Katie thought we should get in and get going before anything else went wrong.

Not far from the airport, our cabby turned off of the quick, busy freeway into Manhattan and drove back into Queens.

"Where is he going?" I asked Katie quietly, sensing that something was wrong.

"I don't know, don't worry it will be ok."

She sounded confident.

"I will look and see if I can buy some gas," the cabby said.

No chance, the pumps had all stopped working. They were electrical, and there was no backup power, not even some kind of hand pump. Unbelievable. We drove around Queens, stopping at every gas station we saw. Katie and I tried to relax by chatting about the city. The sidewalks had become a river of people walking into Queens from Manhattan. There was a flood coming, and we were a little on edge.

After a while the cabby stops his car at a nondescript intersection in the middle of Queens, and motions for us to get out.

"I am sorry, I do not have enough gas, what do you want me to do?"

"Well you can't leave us in the middle of Queens!!" Katie screams at him from the top of her lungs, her eyes welling up almost imperceptibly.

"Don't cry, lady, calm down. What do you want me to do?"

"You should have never picked us up in the first place if you didn't have enough gas!" she shouts.

The man is intimidated. I am thankful that Katie is here. I start to think I am a bit easygoing for this city.

"I can take you back to the airport..." the cabby offers halfheartedly.

"Fine, take us back to the airport!"

Then Katie calmed down a little bit. She might have told him that we weren't going to pay him, I don't remember anymore. If she did, it was not a well measured statement, but tensions were high.

The cabby drove for about five more minutes, heading deeper into Queens. The streets were surprisingly free of traffic – I suppose all the cars had piled up in Manhattan. Eventually, he pulled up to the curb beside a police car. I had a premonition of what would happen next, but could not believe it.

The cabby gets out of his car, and we wait.

"What's he doing?"

We have no clue, but a trip back to the airport appears less and less likely.

"Can't you handle this problem yourselves?" the officer says loudly as he walks up to the cab.

"What's the problem here? Can't you handle this yourselves?" he asks again.

"He said he would take us to Manhattan," we tell him.

Another officer walks up on the other side of the cab.

"Look," he says "we have a call that someone is dying. Now we

can either solve your problem and let somebody DIE, or we can go help them. Which is it going to be?"

Katie and I get out of the cab and remove our bags from the trunk. Katie tells the cabby that she wrote down his cab number.

"Fine, lady, fine," he says and drives away.

It was unfortunate that I was moving to New York and not just visiting. I had brought as much with me on the plane as I could. A large backpack weighing about 25lbs, a laptop computer bag weighing about 30lbs., a suitcase weighing about 45lbs., and a large box of wheeled luggage weighing nearly 70lbs. That's 170lbs of bags to lug around, in case you don't want to do the math. I had only briefly visited New York before, a single visit to look at law schools, and even then I had never ventured outside of Manhattan. But I wasn't too scared. The functional word being 'too'.

Katie and I walked down the street, dragging our luggage as best we could. She was carrying several bags as well, but had packed much lighter. There were no pay phones in sight and Katie's cell phone was not getting any signal. I didn't have a cell phone, myself. After a couple of blocks, Katie stopped on a street corner and dropped her luggage.

"Can you watch the bags while I go find a pay phone?" she asked me. "I have a friend in Queens who might be able to help us."

"Sure, no problem."

Standing near me on the corner, after Katie ran to find a phone, were a young Asian man and woman, both about my age. They looked unfriendly and kept staring at me. Which isn't surprising; I was stranded on a street corner in the middle of Queens, nervous, obviously out of place, with six or seven pieces of luggage piled around me, more on my shoulders, and with a massive river of people teeming down the street behind. The man walked over and said in a thick accent, but with apparently excellent English,

"What happened?"

I gave them the rundown of events, starting out cautiously, but relaxing as I began to sense their genuine concern.

"Oh no!" they both said, with surprise. "He just kicked you out of the cab? That's terrible."

"Do you want to use my cell phone?" the man asked kindly.

"Your cell phone is working??"

"Sure, works fine."

"Wow, great, actually my friend knows someone in the area that she was trying to call. She'll be back in just a minute, I'm sure she will want to use the phone."

"Ok, no problem."

The two of them were some of the nicest people I have met in the city. They tried to reassure me and help me calm down a little bit while we waited for Katie to get back. What I had first interpreted as suspicious gawking, turned out to be just two kind hearted people trying to make sure I was ok.

Katie arrived back quickly.

"Great, I got ahold of her and she lives just a couple blocks away," she told me, with buoyed spirits. "She can hold onto our bags for us. Let's go!"

"Great!" I said, "This fellow was just offering to let us use his cell phone which is still working, apparently."

"New Yorkers are so nice!" Katie exudes.

I said goodbye to the Asian couple, and moved quickly

to follow Katie who was walking up the street as fast as she could go. Her friend's apartment was not too far away. The elevators in the building weren't working, of course, so we had to climb up four flights of stairs with our bags. By the top I was pretty exhausted, and pretty sweaty. I remembered that I was already thirsty when I got off the plane, and hadn't had anything to drink for hours.

As we walk down the hallway we hear high pitched whining, moans, and screams coming from the rooms around us. Like in a horror movie. The hallway is dirty and dark. We knock on the door at the end of the hall and Katie's friend lets us in, her name is Mona. The apartment lives up to a frightening stereotype. You might see something like it in movies depicting New York ghettos — tiny, cramped, dingy, dusty, cluttered, with laundry lines running through the living room. I suddenly feel very privileged, with my nice clothes and brand new luggage. Simultaneously I feel ashamed: Katie's friend is a public school teacher — this is a school teacher's home in Queens.

Mona was an intelligent, down to earth woman who had devoted her life to teaching in an inner-city elementary school. She apologized for the mess and offered us both some water. We chatted with her a little bit, and Katie went back to the bathroom to change clothes. They then briefly discussed events at their elementary school. They told me it was one of the worst inner-city schools in Queens. Even though the stories were about eight-year-olds, none of them were uplifting.

Mona's daughter arrived home from work at some point and squeezed into the apartment. She was a bright, well adjusted woman in her early 20s. Mona had obviously worked hard to make things right for her daughter, and we chatted for a minute about the daughter's plans to attend law school. Naturally, I squeezed in a plug for my own law school. I hadn't yet learned it was a piece of shit.

Mona was pleasant, and she offered to watch our bags until the city calmed down. She didn't say it, but squeezing in all that luggage, let alone extra people, would be a strain on her already cramped living space; we knew we had to move on. Katie and I grabbed our most important bags and steeled ourselves for the hike into Manhattan. Katie had one duffle bag which she slung over her shoulders. I had my large backpack and my computer bag, about 55 lb total weight (I briefly contemplated trying to wheel my largest bag with me, but decided not to.) I really didn't appreciate how far we were from our apartments in Manhattan. We stepped back outside onto the sidewalk and began our march towards the river of people.

I wish I'd had a chance to drink more water.

The exodus of people teeming down the street into Queens had grown while we were inside. Weaving our way through the throngs, Katie and I joined a small trickle of individuals heading the opposite way, in the direction of Manhattan.

We walk a mile or so. It's hot. I sweat like mad. The humidity is unbearable. We see a bus with just enough room left for us to squeeze in. No fares today, everyone who can fit is welcome. The air conditioning feels so good, if only there were an empty seat to sit down. But no, we are crammed in like meat, and I still have two heavy bags on my shoulders. I try to lean back and inadvertently mash someone's hand, who objects angrily. The bus moves very slow. Five or six blocks, and about an hour later, we get off at the first opportunity. Last ones on and first ones off. A couple of sidewalk travelers sprint over to take our place. We have already lost a couple of miles, and want to get to our apartments before dark.

Katie and I walked on through Queens for three or four more miles, but it didn't seem too exhausting. We were catching our second, or maybe our third, wind and our spirits were picking up. This was a great adventure. We talked continuously along the way, there was a subtle charge of chemistry between us, and the crowds of people moving past were incredible to watch. The river of people, and I have no other way to describe it, looked for all the world like an historical exodus, the kind you see in news photos of war torn countries. Eventually, Katie and I made it to the Queensboro Bridge (into Manhattan), where the great, flowing, human body was crossing the East River. Like Israelites and the Red Sea, it was something to behold. Hundreds of thousands of people, perhaps millions. The endless throngs marching from Manhattan into Queens grew larger as we went, and engulfed one side of the bridge completely. The stream trickling into Manhattan became a river of its own. On our side it was a bit smaller of a river, thank heavens.

Our walk across the bridge seems interminable. The first half is all uphill. A rollerblader skates effortlessly past us and weaves his way through the crowd. A bicyclist has worse luck, and is forced to get off and walk. On the other side of the bridge, two unbelievably loud Harley Davidson motorcycles roar slowly past on their way into Queens. You can hear them coming from at least a mile away, and the crowd parts miraculously, as if Moses were standing there stretching out his divine rod and commanding it. Nobody even seems to get squashed in the process.

"Those guys came here on purpose, just to drive by like that," I tell Katie as the engine noise subsides.

"No doubt," she concurs.

The view of the East River from the bridge is incredible. The sun

*is setting, the water is a rich, gem-like, greenish blue, the grass is radi-
ant along the water's edge, and there is a pretty island there in the
middle of it, with pretty, modern buildings that seem to have materi-
alized from out of some Utopian dream.*

*The weight of the bags on my shoulders begins to really hurt me,
and I almost can't put one foot in front of the other by the time we
finish crossing the bridge, but we reach Manhattan.*

59th Street. I thought it would be closer.

*My apartment is on 11th Street, and Katie's is even further
south than that. A tv crew at the entrance of the bridge is filming the
people teeming past. An older man in a yarmulke shouts to them that
he has walked all the way from Flushing Meadows in Queens.*

"Wow," Katie tells me "that's even farther than we came."

*I wonder if he has as far to walk as we still have, and hope he
doesn't.*

The traffic in Manhattan was bumper to bumper. Of
course it was impossible to get a cab. We did get on a bus
again at some point.

*Crushed up against Katie on the bus, crushed together in the
midst of this long ordeal, it suddenly seems natural to reach out and
touch her. To embrace her, and cling to her. I don't go that far. As if
the physical distance between us has been erased, as if we have been
joined together. Touching her feels like touching my own body. This
makes me uncomfortable. We lean against each other for a moment,
and it feels the most natural thing in the world. So much so that it is
disconcerting. I can see in her eyes that Katie is feeling the same thing,
and confused by it. It feels so good to lean against someone. I can
barely stand. My knees give out and I sink halfway to the floor,
crashing against the bus door which springs half open. I pull myself
back upright. Katie looks at me with concern. Embarrassed, my pride
takes over. I force my body to attention and pull my face up into a
mask of strength. We don't lean against each other anymore.*

Again, the bus was even slower than walking, with no possibility of sitting down, and we got off when we could. Again, the last ones on and first off. Darkness was approaching quickly in Manhattan. Crowds had gathered outside every bar, drinking great quantities of alcohol, laughing, enjoying themselves. We couldn't identify with them. Alcohol was available in abundance, but there was nowhere to get any water, as there had been runs on all the shops. The few places selling hydrating beverages had hour long lines waiting just to get inside. We were desperate to get to our apartments before dark, and marched stubbornly on.

A police officer had summed it up best when we asked him if the streets would be safe:

"After dark?" he said with a hard laugh. "After dark? Once the lights go out, nobody knows."

Somewhere around 30th Street, Katie and I find a delicatessen with only a small line in front of it. We must have fluids, having sweated litres, so we join the line. We quickly make it inside the shop, but almost regret this accomplishment immediately. The heat inside is incredible, well into the 100s; it feels exactly like a sauna. I ask for two Snapples, the closest thing to water they are offering. Katie chooses two Sprites. It costs us $6 — a slightly inflated price, but we aren't complaining. Just to accomplish this tiny transaction takes 15 or 20 minutes, standing inside, dying of heat and exhaustion.

We rush back outside as quickly as humanly possible and continue walking. I gulp down one of the Snapples as slowly as I can stand, fearing that I will throw it all up if I drink too fast. The fluid is refreshing. It makes me nauseous. Those don't seem mutually exclusive. I hold the other Snapple up to my face and neck, trying to lower my body temperature. Katie seems to be doing better than I am. The drinks are very cold. I drink the other Snapple, but become more nau-

seous, and leave a little in the bottom as I toss the jar into a trash can.
The jar seemed so heavy.

Eventually, Katie and I reached a point equidistant between our two apartments. Katie gave me precise directions on how to get to my building, and offered to let me continue walking with her if I didn't feel comfortable, and stay the night. She seemed apprehensive about that option, though, so I made sure she would be ok by herself and headed for my apartment on my own.

It is dark and my mind is not functioning clearly. I am incredibly exhausted and my whole body is on fire.

Six more blocks.

I walk past Union Square and vaguely notice NYU hipster kids laying around all over the park. They seem so comfortable. I notice them only momentarily, but envy them profoundly. An animal-like envy I have never experienced before. Like I would kill them and take their place in life right now if I could. I find myself whining and cursing under my breath. Oblivious to the people around me, my vision is tunneled and I can only perceive what is directly in front of my eyes. Four more blocks. I turn and begin walking down 5th Avenue. The cursing grows loud and comes in a steady stream; I remember that normally I never swear. Suddenly I realize that I am going to be very sick when I get to my apartment. I have never been this exhausted or hot before. My heart beats a drumroll, faster than 220 beats per minute, faster than I can count, if I can think enough to count.

I steel myself and stop cursing as I come to the apartment building. Dimly, I discern people sitting outside in front, and that a few of them are holding glow sticks.

"Is this the Cardozo housing?" I say in a thick, labored voice, to no one in particular.

"Yeah, it is."

"Are you the guy that walked all the way from La Guardia?"

"Yeah, that's me," I try to chuckle, but can't.

The superintendent checks me in. Everything is hazy and surreal. He has some forms for me to sign and gives me my keys. I can barely stand. I almost drop my bags and slide down against the wall in the lobby, but painfully manage to hold my body under control. He points me to the appropriate staircase and tells me how to get to my apartment. It's on the 8th floor.

Eight flights of stairs doesn't seem like very much compared to the rest of my journey, but in the back of my mind an insistent voice whispers, "This is not good." I heave my bags back onto my shoulders and start up the stairs.

On the third floor I start cursing again. On the sixth floor I almost collapse. On the seventh floor I almost collapse again. And on the 8th floor I shout something, random words, maybe not even words, hoping someone will come check on me. Nobody comes.

I manage to get into my apartment, where I throw my bags onto the floor and tear my shirt off. The windows are closed, and I slam them open to cool the room off and get some fresh air. The room is completely empty except for a wooden chair and a small table. I try to sit on the chair but can't. I don't know why I can't. I contemplate laying down on the floor and going to sleep.

One of the few wise voices left in my head tells me not to lay down. I realize that I am in trouble, and head back downstairs to try to get to some other people. I almost collapse on every floor and nearly every step, but make my way down quickly. I'm sure I will be ok in a few hours, but want someone to be able to call an ambulance if I pass out. I am trying desperately not to pass out.

I reach the entrance of the building, where the drunk, stressed students outside greet me laughingly as "The Shirtless Wonder". I cannot think clearly to tell anyone what is wrong. I still want to believe I will be ok. I hunch down, sitting, in the middle of the side-

walk for a few minutes, then move back to the entranceway.

"Does anyone have any water I can have?" I ask desperately, barely able to talk.

Some nice girl on the first floor directs me to her apartment, which is lit by candles, and tells me to drink as much as I want. I drink a glass of water, then feel very sick. I walk back to the entranceway and find a seat just outside the door.

Shivering, but terribly overheated, my breaths come fast. I develop an incredible headache. Some time goes by. The superintendent notices that I am not ok, and offers me some water. I accept. He gives me a water bottle. In the back of my mind I realize that I need salt to digest the water, and I ask him if he has anything salty that I can eat. All he has is table salt, so I have him pour a little into my hand. I stick my tongue into the salt and immediately regret it. Then I poor some of the salt into the water and drink a few ounces. I can't drink any more without vomiting. My stomach just can't tolerate it. I sit down again in front of the building.

My breaths come very fast now. I whimper occasionally, but try not to. My head is exploding with pain, wrenching pain that is difficult to believe. My arms, legs, and head turn numb and start to tremble. I realize somewhere in my mind that I am not 'going to be ok', but cannot connect the dots enough to ask for help. A security guard sees that I am in trouble.

"Are you ok, guy?" he asks, "You don't look so good. Let me get you some water."

He gets me a fresh bottle of water which I sip on, having finished most of the other one.

"You going to be ok, buddy?" he asks. "Want me to call an ambulance?"

"I think... I'll be ok," I manage to say, but doubt the words.

"Listen, I'm going to be over here on this corner. If it gets worse or you aren't going to be ok, then tell someone to come get me and I'll

call an ambulance or carry you to the hospital or something."

"Ok," I say.

I cannot express how grateful I am.

I have no comprehension of the passing time. Minutes seem like hours and hours seem to pass without my noticing. I sit hunched over in front of the building. My head hangs inches from the ground. The security guard comes again and says I don't look like I am going to be ok. He calls an ambulance.

"Just at least let them check you out," he says, "Let them check your blood pressure and stuff."

It seems like some of the other students are concerned. Some drunk guy says I am just high and he will carry me upstairs to sleep it off, but people tell him to shut up.

My body starts convulsing. All the muscles in both legs clench up into balls; it feels like a prolonged electric shock, intensely painful. After five or ten minutes the muscles in my legs relax a little. Then all the muscles in my torso clench. Starting in my fingers, the muscles contract uncontrollably and the water bottle flips out of my hand. My arms clench into two bent bars, clench so hard I am afraid the bones will break. I can feel tremendous pressure on my ribs from the muscles in my chest and back. My neck twists until my head looks awkwardly to the side, almost behind me. Although entirely involuntary, it is the most intense physical exertion that I have ever experienced. I breath hard and fast as if I were sprinting, or just finishing a very hard race. Three security guards are watching me. I am sure they can see my muscles twitch violently in the glow of their flashlights. After 15 minutes or so, all my muscles abruptly relax. Relief washes over me like a gentle wave.

"I think I'm going to be ok now," I tell the guards.

The first guard insists that I must wait for the ambulance and let them check me out. The three of them discuss the possibility of taking me to the hospital themselves, which their supervisor has ordered them NOT to do. The first guard places a wet towel over my shoulders to try to cool me off. The towel feels hot.

An hour or two pass after the guards call the ambulance. Their supervisor continues to order them not to take me to the hospital themselves. My muscles go into spasms again. It does not affect my legs as much this time, but is worse in my upper body.

"He's doing that seizure thing again," one of the guards says.

The first guard decides that he is going to take me to the hospital regardless of his supervisor's orders.

"Can you walk, buddy?" he asks.

I can walk a little. He helps me up, holding one contorted arm over his shoulder so that I can lean on him, and putting his other arm around my waist. Without the help I can only stumble directionlessly. Another guard walks with us, holding a flashlight so that we can see where we are going. The third guard stays behind to keep an eye on the apartments.

The hospital was only three avenue blocks away. Doctors in the emergency room checked me in, made sure my blood pressure and pulse were ok, and sent me in a wheelchair to 'recovery' for dehydration treatment. I thanked the two guards as best I could, still barely able to talk, and they returned dutifully to their posts at the student housing.

The doctors lay me in a bed, stick me with an IV, and run a litre of fluid into my blood as quickly as they can. Then they run a second litre of fluid into me. Then a third litre. After the third they are taken aback.

"Don't you need to use the bathroom?" they keep asking.

"No. ...Why?"

"Normally, after 1 or 2 litres people need to pee like a racehorse," one of the doctors says.

They pump a fourth and then a fifth litre into me, with the valve on the IV completely open. I still don't really need to use the bathroom, but I force myself to anyway because they are afraid my lungs might start filling up with fluid. It is a good sign that I am able to get up and walk to the bathroom on my own, wheeling my IV. One of the doctors says that I was so dried out he is "surprised your veins were still functioning enough to take an IV."

My skin becomes puffed and pasty. I feel blown up like a balloon. I'm scared to have any more fluid pumped into my veins, and feeling much, much better, although I have an incredible headache and am quite weak. My mind is not quite all together. The doctors stop the fluid treatments and I gradually fall asleep.

I think it was 1 a.m. or 2 a.m. by the time I fell asleep in the hospital. I drifted in and out of sleep throughout the night.

The headache is bad, but gets steadily better. I am completely exhausted. No, that's not true. I am profoundly spent, frayed to the single fibres of my being. The doctors and nurses check on me regularly. St. Vincent's hospital is running entirely on backup systems because of the blackout, and everyone goes the extra mile to make things work. The care is so impressive I almost think they could bring a person back from the dead. I sleep more.

Sometime in the early morning I was awoken by the gentle touch of a nurse's hand against my arm. A tall, pretty, black American woman, she wore a serious and sympathetic look on her face. She explained to me that they had gotten my blood tests back. Apparently, my body had started breaking down its muscle tissues and converting them into fluid. This was the cause of my convulsions. Two different blood tests, taken hours apart, had come back at the same time, and the second was worse than the first.

Which meant the process was accelerating. My kidneys, she said, were in danger of clogging up and failing.

The doctors put me back on fluid IV, but at a slower drip rate. I would be taking continuous intravenous fluids for the rest of my stay in the hospital, keeping my system flushed to prevent my kidneys from clogging.

"You're going to have to be checked in," the nurse says to me.

"What does that mean?"

"You can't stay here," she says, with a note of regret in her voice, "this area is for people who are getting better and are going home soon."

I look at her blankly.

"There are no rooms available right now, because of the outage," she continues, "but you're going to move upstairs to a hospital ward as soon as one becomes available."

She was a very kind woman and didn't enjoy telling me this. All the doctors and nurses in that room were the same way: very kind, and hyper-competent. Many of them had been working more than 24 hours straight, and some took cat naps in the corners after finishing their necessary tasks. I was shocked, though, that I was going to have to stay another night in the hospital. I was feeling much better, no more headache, and had thought I could go home in a few more hours at the most.

Early the next afternoon I was visited in the emergency room by some of the administrators at my law school. They were the first people, who knew who I was, to find out where I was and what had happened to me. They were also the first who were able to contact my family and let them know what had happened. And the only visitors I had in the hospital, since I didn't know anyone in New York.

Late in the afternoon, the power came back on at the

hospital and I was moved to a ward on the sixth floor. My roommates here were an old Asian man who was completely bed ridden, and a middle aged Polish fellow with an indecipherable accent who seemed perfectly healthy, but was waiting to be transferred to another hospital for a month long stay. Staff kept asking if I was, "the guy who walked all the way from La Guardia?" One young doctor was particularly pleased to finally meet me. "Everyone in the hospital is talking about your story," he said.

On the second night they took my blood again, and it was again worse. They had taken blood 4-5 times and each result came back worse than the last. The doctors said that the decomposition of my muscles was leveling off, though. Apparently, this muscle break down was a process that, once begun, was difficult for the human body to put a stop to.

The following morning I felt much better. Good as new. The doctors took another blood sample. It seemed as though I had been in the hospital forever, although it had only been two nights. I was anxious to find out what happened to my luggage and retrieve it so that I could change clothes, take a shower, and generally start putting my life back together. By 10 a.m. that morning I was so antsy I started peeling at my IV, sorely tempted to tear it off and just walk away. I told all of the staff, in no uncertain terms, that I wanted to leave ASAP. Eventually, I calmed down and waited more patiently. In the afternoon they finally got my latest blood work back and it had improved. My body was finally repairing itself, instead of doing the opposite; I was on the up and up. The doctor on duty checked me out at 4 p.m., with instructions to drink "lots and lots" of fluids and take it easy for a while.

As I was being checked out, I asked a nurse what to do with the hospital gown I had been wearing over my shoulders, and if it would be ok for me to walk out of the hospital with no shirt. The staff all got a big laugh out of this, and I had to smile too. Only the people in the emergency room knew that I had arrived at the hospital without a shirt on. The nurses found me a nice, clean shirt that some kind heart had donated for such an eventuality. It's one of my favorites now.

When I got back to my apartment I borrowed an old phone from the building superintendent only to discover that Verizon had not activated my phone line like they were supposed to. I went back downstairs and borrowed the super's cell phone to call Katie. I was a bit worried about her, especially after my own ordeal.

Katie said that she was just fine, she had had a mild headache after our odyssey, but that was the extent of it. She was very sorry to hear of my travails. Katie had already collected our bags from Mona, so I made a quick cab trip over to her apartment to pick up my bags.

It was strange to see Katie again. There is a peculiar bond of intimacy that springs up between people thrown together in traumatic situations, even total strangers, and I don't think either of us was quite comfortable with it. She let me use her phone to call Verizon, whose automated system informed me they had activated my phone line at precisely 9:32 p.m. on the night of the blackout. Some kind of joke. Katie helped me carry my bags downstairs and catch a cab back to my apartment.

I lugged all 120lbs of bags up to my apartment (using the elevator this time), and finally took a sorely needed shower. I lay down for a little while, and then went and found change and a pay phone for some long calls home to family. The next morning my brother, studying a half day's drive away in Ithaca, NY, caught a bus into the city to help me set-up the apartment and recuperate. It was nice to see a familiar face. That's less than the truth.

It took me a few weeks to really start recovering my vigor. Several months of hard work was required to regain the physical strength I had lost. I guess the bright side of the whole thing was that I had a great story to tell all the new people I met in the weeks following the blackout. The story was a guaranteed mind blower, and as long as I laughed while I told it, which I always did, it somehow left a good impression.

I tried to keep in touch with Katie. I called her, anyway, and left a message on her machine. She never called me back. It's peculiar how a few stressful hours like that can have such a dramatic impact on your life. When you're tossed into such an intense situation with another person it's something that nobody else outside of it can quite understand or really share. It inspires an undeserved intimacy. Maybe that's the problem for well grounded minds, or why some will cling to that intimacy after the trauma has abated. Undeserved, but natural, even primeval. And if it's a young man and woman thrown together then that's even more complicated, isn't it? Because in that moment, the intimacy becomes physical. I don't think either of us were quite at ease with that foundation, and we haven't kept in touch. I still have her number, though, and every once in a while I look at it and think about dialing again. I imagine chatting about the day of the blackout.

New York settled naturally into me, and this is why: I

almost died when I came here. After that I didn't have time to worry about how I liked the city or how I fit in, or any of the endless other things that might have distracted or upset. I didn't have time to waste 'getting to know' New York. I was here, and I was weak and recovering, and by the time I could worry about anything else it all felt normal. That night of the blackout became a crossroads. In some forbidden wilderness of time. When I lay dying in New York, somehow my life started over. And I became a New Yorker.

CHAPTER 2

IN THE PINPRICK space between forest leaves, if Adam had looked to see, there was now an occasional smudge of orange. Sometimes yellow or black. Sometimes, if Adam had looked, a hard eye staring back at him. Catching his scent off of the air, and following.

Adam leapt over a stream, very nearly unimpeded by his packs and tools. He chirruped at a bird atop a bush, which flew twittering away in a flash of red and blue. Too quickly. He heard an easy thump, like a soft padded foot upon the ground. Not far off.

Had he really heard it?

He set down his things, moving quietly towards the half-heard something lost on the air. Maneuvering through the underbrush, the green foliage, ferns, weeds, miniature flowers, the thick with life around him. Reading the air, the scents and winds and feel of it, the thickness of it on his skin. His eyes took in the waver of each leaf, the blades of grass, the little insects here and there, working as they were. Softly lit in the distance, on a low rise across the falling stream, a stag stared down at him.

The stag stood proudly, its heavy rack lifted high into the air. Staring, challengingly. Staring. Adam could see tension in the creature's muscles, the flared muzzle, upturned ears, the bigness of its eyes. He understood what it is for a deer to stare, an herbivorous creature whose eyes are not made to look directly ahead.

"Easy, King, I mean no harm," Adam said softly to

himself. He whistled a fragment of an old lullaby his mother had sung to him, letting the notes catch upon the breeze and be carried away. "Easy, King, we're the same you and me."

The breeze blew up over the hill, carrying the lullaby in a whispering, damp, ethereal blanket. Wrapping up the stag, familiar, soaking him, and bleeding off, and whistling on. The stag whipped his head and bounded off. Adam lifted his bags back onto his shoulders and continued along his path. The red-blue lark was back, higher in the trees now, clicking and screeching at him.

Not far off, the soft-padded feet lifted again, ever so quietly, stalking Adam through the forest. A long, spotted tail curled quietly around, brushing away flies, whipping aside leaves and tangled vines. If you stood close enough, you could hear the low rumble in its chest. If you could get down on the ground and follow it, watch as it lifted one of its heavy feet, you could see the claw marks, shallow, retracted, ticked off one by one in the soft earth.

Adam came to a clearing in the wood. The noonday sun felt good upon his face. He set down his packs and tools in the center of it, where the sky's bright rays washed over him seductively. He thought about making his garden here. No, the earth was too dry. He would find someplace better. He retrieved a slice of mana from his food pack and climbed onto the remains of a fallen tree, sitting atop the broken trunk and beginning his meal.

Golden eyes glinted in the sun at the edge of the clearing, burning into Adam's back, reflecting his figure onto itself. The low rumble from their chest was louder now. Their lips curled back and quivered, introducing fangs into the raw forest air.

Prickling, thick belly hairs brushed the forest floor as

the beast inched its way into the clearing. Its pupils contracted precisely, mechanically, in the sunlight, yet remained large. Step by step, inch by inch, coiled low against the ground, it crept. Adam sat eating his meal. Twenty yards ahead. Fifteen... Ten yards...

A deep, carnivorous scream pierced and petrified the air.

Blood flooded powerfully into Adam's brain, numbing, clouding. With a violent exercise of will, he forced his body into an awkward spin. For one frozen moment in time he saw the leopard leaping off of the ground. Then its excremental breath exploded across his face. Blackness flashed over his consciousness.

An enormous paw, five long, extended claws, tore heavily across Adam's chest. The scent of blood lit the air. Adam wrapped his legs instinctively around the leopard's long body and they tumbled to the ground. A fang sank into his shoulder. Twisting away, he slid onto the beast's side, and locked his limbs around it like a python.

The leopard thrashed and rolled across the ground, crushing Adam against unforgiving earth. Small, sharp stones. Saw-like green nettles now wet with blood. Night flashed on and off in Adam's eyes. The world became unsteady, and lost its focus. He realized he was about to die. And revolted against the thought.

Seizing the leopard's nearest leg with both hands, Adam wrenched desperately in the wrong direction. With a crunch, the leg gave way and the leopard squealed in pain. It tried to pull away from Adam, who kicked off of it, sprinting for the tools in the center of the clearing. The leopard leapt after him. Its injured leg collapsed and it tumbled heavily into the ground.

Air shook again as the beast rose slowly back onto its

feet. Lacking the benefit of confidence or surprise, the sonic weapon quavered, impotent. Head down, the leopard limped menacingly forward.

Adam picked up his sharp, heavy stone shovel and lifted it high overhead. His eyes shone now, bright and dangerously. He stood proudly, like an ancient hero, battered and bloodied under a ferocious sun. Glared down at the cruel, killing monster lumbering towards him, breathing heavily, picking up its pace.

"Hyaaahhaaa!" Adam rushed forward with a primal, animal cry, sound divorced from reason. The leopard lunged to meet him. Stopping short, Adam swung the shovel in a great arc, sweeping grey against the blue sky, and buried it in the leopard's ribs.

The leopard stopped, still, and snorted violently. He wrenched his shovel from the beast's flesh and raised for another strike. It was already retreating. Incomprehensibly fast now, on its three good legs, the monster disappeared back into the forest as quickly as it had come.

A great, sudden stillness filled the clearing. Like a storm that existed had suddenly been erased. All that remained were sticky trails of blood to bear witness to the battle. And a beautiful, wounded manchild collapsing to the earth.

flute and clarinet duet. andante.

This is just a random, ordinary kind of thing, a 'slice of life' if you will. I call it "the usual".

I'M WALKING DOWN the street in front of my apartment building, carrying bags from the grocery store. It's a sunny, spring day. Beautiful. Some good rock music flows from a nearby rooftop, it sounds like someone is playing a gig. I think of the Beatles and their famous impromptu roof concert in New York. Is this a once in a lifetime experience? Something special? Or just high quality speakers pumping air through a penthouse window?

In front of my building is a pretty girl about my own age. Brunette, medium height, cute little build, in fancy jeans, sneakers, and kind of a horizontal striped, figure hugging, knit blouse. She is sitting on the steps, just hanging out. Listening to the music. I've never seen her before, and wonder if I could possibly have overlooked such an attractive neighbor.

"That music sounds really good," I say to her as I walk up to the steps.

"Isn't it? I had to stop and listen for a minute," she says.

"Oh, do you live in the building here?"

"No," she laughs, "no, I was just walking by."

"Ah, darn," I say, sitting down on the steps beside her. "I was hoping you were one of my neighbors."

She laughs again and surveys me curiously. Doesn't seem uncomfortable with the fact I have sat down beside her.

"So what is that, a concert or something?"

"I think it's just somebody's speakers turned up really loud," she says.

"Yeah, maybe. It sounds so real, though."

"Yeah."

"Made me think of the Beatles."

"Haha, yeah."

We chat randomly for a few minutes. She is heading over to Cooper Union to meet up with some friends. She wonders about myself, what I "do", not what I'm doing.

"Yeah, I'm a law student, actually."
"Oh, NYU?"

Why do they always say that?

"No. Uh, Cardozo?" I put it as a question to see if she has even heard of the place. Hoping to sound nonchalant and not defensive.
"..."
"It's just here around the corner."
"Oh. How do you like law school?"
"Do I like it?" I ask, hoping the question will change.
"Yeah, how do you like it?"
"Um… No, I don't like it."
I know it's a mistake to say, but just can't bring myself to lie. She looks at me a little disappointed, like I'm not as much as she hoped and I just broke social etiquette on top of that. I mean, I don't mean to say it in a bad way, to be negative or whatever. I just happen to hate law school with a consuming passion. The best positive spin I can put on it is to say I don't really like it. I don't like to talk about it, to tell you the truth.
"Well, you know," I say, trying harder, "it's ok. It's just not really the thing for me."
"Then why are you there?"
Maybe I should be flattered by her interest, but already it's taken a critical tone. Not friendly, like we are on the same level, but more like 'Maybe I can help you with your

problems within the next thirty seconds of our conversation.' Which I really don't resent, I'm not so cynical, just that it is counterproductive to any romantic feelings between a man and a woman who just met. That's my opinion.

"Why am I there? Stubbornness, I guess. You know, it's not so bad, I've only got one more year left at this point. What do you do?"

"You really don't seem like a law student," she says, her manner changing almost imperceptibly. I smile, and relax

"That's what people tell me," I say conspiratorially, as if we are both on the same page now. I imagine my eyes sparking with romance as I say it. She leans towards me and gives off a little half laugh, about to say something, but I'm quicker.

"Well, what do you do then? Don't try to dodge the question."

"I'm not dodging," she blinks her eyes demurely in mock defense, "I'm in publishing."

"Really, publishing? What do you do? In publishing, I mean."

"I work in children's books. Working with writers, that sort of thing," she says vaguely.

"Like editing?"

"Yeah, sort of."

I wonder how one ends up in that kind of work? If you're not a writer, I mean. Like, do you just have to stumble into it? You probably have to know somebody. Even if you're a writer. Imagine working in the children's book industry, how much fun it could be. It could be the best job ever.

"Ok, I have a question for you," I say. "What's the deal with all these celebrity children's books now?"

"What do you mean?"

"It just seems like this big new phenomenon of the children's book written by some celebrity – where does it come from?"

"Well, they sell. People buy them."

I usually think before I speak. Most people don't, did you ever notice that? Why don't they? But when someone doesn't, I guess I try to make them think. It's my own little style of manipulation.

"I don't know," I say easily, "it just seems like children's books are a pretty important thing and maybe random celebrities aren't the best people to write them. What do you think, would you have your kids reading Madonna's children's book?"

"Well, some are better than others. Yeah, I dunno, probably not. The celebrities don't really write them anyway."

"Ah, right," I chuckle. "So you write them, then?"

"What?"

Noise from a construction crew down the street momentarily drowns out our conversation. I lean closer to her, so that our cheeks are almost touching, so just for a passing moment she can feel my breath against her ear and neck.

"I said, so you write them then?"

"Hahaha, no, not me." She smiles at me. "No, I'm not much of a writer. I do all the other stuff."

"I'm sure you're a better writer than you think."

"…Mmmm… No," she says, smiling again.

We chat for a few more minutes and nothing much remarkable happens. We talk about the city, about Greenwich Village, about her work and my school. Soon she says she has delayed too long and must be on her way.

"Hey, would you like to have a cup of coffee with me later?" I ask as she stands up.

"Coffee?"

"Yeah, coffee, whatever. I just, you know, wish we could get more of a chance to talk."

She is already walking away, trying to get away. Why?

"Well, maybe I'll see you around sometime," she says.

"Yeah, maybe."

She turns her back to me, a dozen paces away now.

"Take it easy," I call after her.

She turns her face, without breaking stride, and dignifies me with a quick half-wave of goodbye.

CHAPTER 3

ADAM DID NOT wake until evening. Dizzily, in the starlight, he dragged himself to a cold stream and gulped water. Cleaned and bandaged his wounds as best he could. He crawled back to the clearing and collapsed again, and woke feverishly in the afternoon sun the next day. Forcing himself to his feet, he took to the woods. His mind was fibrous, cottony. Sometimes it wasn't there at all. He tried to follow his map, but became hopelessly lost.

Over the next few days, Adam slowly returned to his senses. He was uncommonly strong, even for a man of York. The small cuts and abrasions all over his body were healing nicely. Claw wounds across his chest less so, but they were healing. He was still in the forest, it was the same as it had been, the same forest he knew well, but... different.

These woods were ancient, untouched. It was something about the thickness of the bark on the trees, and the undergrowth, the set of the forest. There had never been any garden here. No grown-over gardens like in the woods near York. It was strange to notice the difference. Foreboding. These woods were denser. How far from York had he wandered?

Adam proceeded in a line through the forest, charting his direction with the sun when he could peek through the branches to see it. He traveled cautiously, less confident, lest he meet any more legendary creatures like the leopard. After a while, he found a quick running stream cutting through the thick woods and followed it, hoping to arrive at some lake or river that he would recognize.

The stream tumbled acrobatically through ancient groves of trees and ageless plants. Sometimes Adam had to wade through the water itself to pass. These plants were the same ones he was accustomed to. The same forest creatures. Mostly. Occasionally he saw something new, but mostly they were the same. It was hard to say what was different about these woods. They were just – more virgin. Less interrupted. Not for the past year, ten years, or the past hundreds, but for ages and ages past. Something about the pattern was changed. Something more free, chaotic. Maybe it was just the smell, an absence of passing humanity. Maybe a thing like that lingers for years, and you would never know it, you would only notice when it was gone.

Rounding a sharp bend in the stream, after following it for half of a day, Adam came upon ancient brickwork. He stared at it uncomprehendingly at first, buried in the foliage as it was. His jaw fell slowly open, until it gaped wide. This was made by human hands. This was an ancient, crumbling *building*. Once recognized, the intricate brickwork was still beautiful to behold, even without wooden ornaments and fixtures that had long since rotted away. It was a tall, elegant building, what remained, somewhat delicately conceived. Not at all like the heavy, solid architecture of York. Vines and creeping flowers crawled across the roof and fell about it. Adam peered inside, but the building was ages past deserted. Perhaps thousands of years ago.

"People lived here," Adam said to himself wonderingly.

He pushed his hand through a tangle of vines and rested it against the moss covered wall.

A mile more downstream, the woods opened onto a vast deserted city. For all that nature had encroached on it in intervening centuries, still spectacular to behold. The buildings were all constructed of that same intricate brick-work Adam had discovered in the forest, but here were the remains of towers and cathedrals, massive columns dotted around ancient courtyards, scatter colored mosaic tiles that still betrayed hints of their epic images. Enormous marble statues gazed down upon the empty cobbled streets, features eroded, skin pitted, arms and legs and heads missing, for all that, maintaining their watch.

Adam stood and stared in wonder from the distance, moving out of the woods and up to the crest of a small hill. He blinked his eyes at the monumental discovery, hardly believing that this reality could be real.

The ancient ruins called to Adam, and he wandered through them. Trying to imagine a city and civilization other than York. He scarcely could. In York, other peoples and civilizations existed only as mythology. Fantasy tales to dazzle children. York was timeless, unchanging and untouched. As far as anyone knew, or would confess to know, things had always been as they were, and always would be. There was no exploration or invention. Hardly any imagination. These were not part of the culture. Everything had its order, every person had their place. There was never any reason to question it. Adam ran through the ancient, ruined streets, and they seemed less a revelation than an incredible dream. An experience that smacked of unreality, from which no conclusions could be readily drawn.

The experience started to overwhelm him, and Adam returned stubbornly to his task at hand. He climbed to the top of a tall, crumbling tower, looking out over the forest to see if he could spot any of the landmarks on his map.

From this vantage point, he could see a lake on the horizon that matched with one outlined on the edge of his map. It took him only a few minutes to gauge its direction and deduce a rough estimate of his current location. For many more minutes he sat staring wild eyed at the magnificent ruins surrounding him. More people must have lived here once, he thought, than in all of York. Or had anyone lived here at all? Perhaps this was one of the faerie cities told of in legend.

A voice drifted up from the distance, startling Adam out of his reverie. Sound of someone singing, a love song, broken up by the wind. The voice was far away, then suddenly close, and Adam could make out the words.

> "And I'll walk among the rarer flowers
> Found on the soft green forest floor,
> And lose myself in those gentle bowers.
> Only my love can find me,
> Forever and ever more."

He looked quickly in every direction, but could not discover the source of the singing. Surely no other man from York had wandered to this far off corner of the forest. What could it possibly be, except for a faerie or a ghost? And what a beautiful, feminine voice — surely a faerie maiden. Adam scrambled down from the tower to discover the source of the song. Reaching the ground, he jogged quietly along a rutted, stone cobbled street, frightened and excited, following the beautiful voice.

> "Bend the green boughs before me
>   and the green trees o'er me,
> Keep the bright sun above me
>   and the warm breeze before me.
> In my life… In my life.

In my life... In my life."

As he rounded a leafy, crumbling, palace corner, off of an ancient grand thoroughfare, the song became abruptly louder. It seemed to materialize in front of him. Before Adam could stop himself he was looking into the eyes of its songstress.

Hypnotized.

Motionless, stammering, unable to break from her gaze. His stomach turned over. His heart raced uncontrollably. He found himself consumed by a desire to move forward, to be closer to this girl. With considerable effort he stopped his feet, a dozen paces away, and simply stared. Breathlessly gazing into her huge, deep green eyes.

"Hello?" she said gracefully, but with sharp challenge in her voice.

Adam did not hear her. Enchanted by her endearing expression of shock, of her mouth caught half-open, frozen, and a note dying on the air. A warmth ran through his blood as he continued to stare. The girl stared back as raptly. Their eyes locked in some strange, embracing, con-testing, challenge of a greeting. Adam willed himself to look away, but could not. Her eyes bored into him, unre-lenting. And he was glad of it. As much as anything, afraid that she would look away. Or even disappear.

"Hello?" she said again, more gently this time, noticing Adam's stammering lips, his confused, unthreatening pos-ture.

"Hello," her voice rang nearly as musical as her song, "who are you? Do you speak?"

"A — are you a faerie?" Adam finally said, floating the words out on a reservoir of pride.

"What?"

"Are you a faerie?" he asked again, firmly this time, but could still not look away from her face.

"No I'm not a faerie! A faerie? It isn't nice to mock somebody you just met, you know. Where do you come from, silly boy?"

Crimson embarrassment welled up in Adam's face, breaking the spell. Before him was a beautiful young woman of about his own age. She had long, brown hair that tangled up in waves as it ran down her back. Finely sewn leathers, which complimented her bronze, burnished skin. A beaded bracelet of black and crimson wrapped itself tightly around her upper arm, and seemed to contradict her bright, deep, incandescent eyes. She was half a head shorter than Adam, and much more delicate, but there was something vaguely imposing about her, something in the way she carried herself. They stood a dozen or so paces apart, although Adam's silence now caused her to slowly, almost imperceptibly, retreat a few steps more.

"Where do you come from?" Adam asked with more confidence.

"I believe I asked you first."

"I come from York, where everybody comes from," he rejoined challengingly. "Why haven't I seen you before? What are you doing outside of the city?"

"Well I hope most men of York have better manners than you, sir."

"What's wrong with my manners?"

"I asked you what your name was – you still haven't told me."

The young woman backed up to a low wall and sat lightly on top of it. Adam followed her lead, sitting down opposite her on a crumbly chunk of boulder, with the ancient, uprooted cobblestones forming a river between them. He conjured an apple from an inner jacket pocket, and cut off and ate a slice of it while the girl watched him.

"Would you like some?" he asked politely.

"Yes," she said quickly, hopping off the wall and advancing partway towards him, then stopping. "I've not had an apple in... a long time. Throw it here."

"You don't have to be afraid of me," Adam said as he sliced the apple in half. "My name's Adam."

She stood motionless, holding out her hands to catch the fruit.

"My name is Eve. Just throw it here, please!"

Adam stared quizzically to one side a moment, then threw half of the apple to her and resumed eating his own. Eve hurried back to her perch on the opposite wall, biting hungrily into the crisp fruit.

"Thank you, Adam."

He watched her curiously, chewing. He spit a seed onto the ground. Eve spit a seed out too, as if in imitation.

"Where did these buildings come from?" Adam asked.

"I don't know, there must have been an enormous city here once. How did you get here, Adam?"

"A city? ...You mean with *people*."

"Of course with people. What do you mean?"

"But... all the people live in York. They always have."

"Who told you that?"

"Everyone knows that."

"I don't know that," Eve said, with the faintest note of scorn in her voice.

"Who ever heard of a person outside of York? This must have been a faerie city," Adam continued insistently.

"I'm not from York. I've never even heard of York. Where is it?"

"You are a faerie, aren't you," Adam said excitedly, swallowing a large chunk of fruit.

"I'm just a girl."

They stared at each other appraisingly.

"York must be very far away; how did you get here, Adam?"

"It's not so far," Adam said, looking at his map again. "Maybe four, five days' walk. I got lost trying to find an old garden that a friend told me about. That's how I ended up here."

Eve watched him, silent.

"But on top of that tower, the tall one over there, I could see a lake on the horizon, and that is on my map. So I know where I am now."

He glanced at her hopefully. Eve watched intently, with a puzzled look on her face, but said nothing.

"When I was up there," Adam continued, "I heard you singing. That's why I came down to find you. I think it was the most beautiful sound I ever heard. Like a faerie song."

"Faeries again," Eve said. Then more softly, "My mother used to sing that song."

"It's beautiful."

"Thank you," she said, looking at the ground. She looked up again, winking, "I don't guess I would have been singing if I knew someone else was here."

"Well, I'm glad you hadn't spotted me, then."

He could not help smiling at her. Tension drained slowly out of Eve's face, and she smiled back.

A Cappella Waltz

                    To set the mood for this next section
you should imagine someone dancing. Ever so gracefully. Not a
waltz, more of a ballet. Or not a ballet.

Ok, never mind, don't imagine that.

To be read aloud:

IT WAS 3 a.m. I looked over, and there was a new couple on the dance floor. Their dance was ridiculous. One could not help but laugh. The man's arms flailed awkwardly, pulled by the strings of some mad puppeteer. The woman – how can I describe it? She danced like nothing I had ever seen before. Caught up in a wild sort of epileptic fervor. Moving chaotically. Dancing entranced. Wrapped up within a joyous seizure. Like nothing I had ever seen before – or since. I stood shocked in awe, and laughed, and watched her movements.

So I asked my friend Samantha, who knows a little more than me, what kind of drugs would allow a girl to dance so inexplicably? And she agreed that she had never seen the like before; it was honestly remarkable.

"I don't know," she said, "but I feel like I should find out."

I was almost thinking the same thing myself; her suggestion left no doubt in my mind as to the appropriate course of action.

"Go ask her," I said, "and don't worry, you can blame me for this infraction."

My friend Samantha wants not for moxie, she walked straight over and asked promptly, asked the strange wild dancing girl, what drugs enabled her chaotic whirl? They talked a moment, smiling. And in the meanwhile I sat entrapped. This dance that had seemed so strange and wrong had me hypnotized, and before long I had come to reverse my previous point of view. In all fairness, this dance was something new, and so you'll please forgive me that I could first but laugh, for on seeing more than the half of it, now bereft of laughter, I found myself entranced quite hopelessly, and realized, beyond chance, this wild whirling dancing dance, this epileptic's grand daydream, was something very special indeed. It was not wrong, there was no plight, it was no chemically altered sight, or state of mind, I have to say, it was strangely right, somehow more than ok.

Samantha returned with the heartening news that my newfound muse had suffered naught but flow of booze, or, so to speak, in her own parlance, "I'm just real drunk and I love to dance!" I would have sworn it was ecstasy. Or something stronger, it was strange, you see. And incredible, and indelible, almost medical, and yet beautiful. I could not look away, I just sat and watched. For at least fifteen minutes on my heart of hearts clock. And suddenly I realized with a start, that this Dancing Girl, this beneficent tart, had another bond to my muse: she was a tall beautiful blonde. The sort of girl, in honesty, I'm more than apt myself to choose.

Now this was really quite amazing, don't pass it by with unjust appraising: I was a young single guy, hot red blooded and a little drunk, in a dancing club that had run amok; the type with his eye out all the night and all the day in much the same way, and I, even I, what unthinkable thing, in my hypnotized state in my mystified wondering, at the glorious dance of that glorious pearl, in the jubilant trance of The Dancing Girl, could not see, not observe, the most glorious curves, and such beautiful face, fine golden hair, oh what grace, could not see not perceive such a beautiful dream, the fair creature embodiment of such beautiful dancing.

I sense you doubt the honest ring of my words, so let me elaborate, that you can collaborate in my ideas, such as they are, or at least such as you perceive. The Dancing Girl was beautiful, of that there can be no doubt. With a model's build, not too skinny though, an elfin face, nice warm glow behind the eyes, even a rosy hue in the cheek; it would be hard to seek a prettier pearl than The Dancing Girl. But even so, hard, aye, yes, but possible, and yet, that other factor still rings more clear: the glorious whirl of the dance: what a sight, what an odds-off outside improbable chance one could ever see another dance like that dance, or even see it once, at that, it's quite amazing in point of fact. And I'm sure you don't yet quite understand, but bear with me yet. It's hard to explain but I'm doing the best I can.

The man she was with was a cheap imitation. The Dancing Girl's dance was a mystical act, a white pure orgy of celebration, a touch of real magic, a true revelation. There was something so primal and honest about it. So uninhibited, unclouded, undoubted, if you watched for a moment you just could not doubt it. No cloying, no tension, no pretense, no stress. There was no reservation, anxiety, distress. No pent up expression, emotion, just some wild beautiful free-flowing whirl of mystical magical physically fantastical, undoubted, undaunted, unconscious, unbowed, blissfully pure flow emotional soul uncut and untamped unleashed and unsheathed unaware of the crowd.

In those few brief moments my heart was seeded, fertilized, watered, weeded, sunned, cross-breeded, gathered, reaped, heaped, and ploughed!

So I did what I had to. I walked straight to her, put my hand on her shoulder, turning her away from her dancing partner, and said, "You're my favorite dancer ever." Which produced a broad smile, and a look in the eye, and a full turn around, with her back to the dancing guy. The next song had started, it was dangerous and brash, but I took that chance, and she liked me for it. A lot. Her dancing man she forgot, our eyes were locked, and she said to me, "Let's dance."

Now things become a bit more serious, or less whimsical would be better said, so I do hope you'll please forgive me, but I simply must change my prosody.

I could never have resisted dancing with The Dancing Girl. I'd go hell and back to do it again. Her energy was infectious, her dance intoxicating – and she was very beautiful. Throw in vintage dancehall hits in the background and you have a recipe for triumph or disaster. For me it was a little bit of both. I began to dance with The Dancing Girl, even while piqued to the real possibility that some jealous lover might attack me.

Oh, but it was, by far and away, the best dancing I had ever had. And I'm a man who loves to dance. As we danced, we exchanged simple pleasantries. Like this:

"You're a great dancer!" she said.

"Thank you, so are you!" I said.

"Where are you from?" she asked.

"I live in New York, in Greenwich Village, what about you?"

"Tribeca."

"Nice.

"Heh, I thought you were with that guy," I said, still watching my back.

"I am."

"Oh, Yeah? 'Cause he seems pretty pissed off."

"It doesn't matter. I can dance with whoever I want."

"...No, really, what's the situation with you two."

"I'm dating him."

"I see."

So I pretty much knew the score at that point. Careful dodging of the word 'boyfriend' isn't hard to decipher. But the night was winding down and I needed to make a fast connection if I ever wanted to see The Dancing Girl again, let alone dance with her. A slow song came on through the loudspeakers, and we started dancing to it, but then an angry young man came walking over to us, and The Dancing Girl got this sad, regretful look on her face.

"Look," she said gripping my arm and imploring me with unbroken eye contact, "I *have* to dance with him for this song, but I want to dance with you more. You're not leaving or anything are you?"

"No, I'll be here a little while longer," I said, staying cool.

Then her boyfriend grabbed hold of The Dancing Girl. It was a mean display, though I can't say that I blame him. Groping her every which way, in mechanical objectification. To assert control of his territory. And I knew she was with him because of his money. Or because of some fame she expected him to have. I can't say how, and you don't have to believe it. I just knew. You could see in her eyes she wasn't happy. And that didn't sit well with me.

A funny thing, is that the man she was dating, her boyfriend I assume, was not the man she'd been dancing with before. It wasn't quite as she had told me, because the man she'd been dancing with was a friend of her date, and her date was the one who finally came over to get her away from me. But strong drink and loud music will often lead to disjointed communications of this sort.

What can I say; that was the last song, the lights came on, and as the bouncers shooed us out the door, The Dancing Girl was locked up tight in her boyfriend's arms. With him and his two male companions glaring at me. You can't exactly go up and ask for a girl's phone number under those circumstances, or even get a friend to go give her your number. I felt a bit winded. Still, it had been a grand night, so I walked smugly out of the door with a smile.

As I stood outside laughing with my friends, The Dancing Girl walked out. Her boyfriend's arms still locked around her, and him still glaring at me. Glaring, still, were his two male companions. But The Dancing Girl locked eyes with me again, locked eyes and smiled. And she gave me this look – something hard to decipher. There was a warmth in it, and a thank you – an I'm sorry, and a regret. And... what was it... a question. That's what it was, there was a question in it. But there was no time for asking or answering questions. I held her gaze for a moment and winked. Her cloister trio turned red in the face.

"Oh shit, there's gonna be a fight," a friend of mine said.

But that wasn't it at all. I turned to join my friends and we walked away.

It had been a magnificent evening even before I met The Dancing Girl. For all of us, I think, not only me. So we walked on down the Village streets, laughing and talking, ready for some last bit of adventure, somewhere or other, before closing out the night.

I don't know why I winked at her. It just seemed the thing to do. But I think about my last communication with The Dancing Girl. Her boyfriend and his friends disgusted me, and I wanted to make them angry. I wanted to be sure they understood that I was neither afraid nor intimidated. If she was using me to make her boyfriend jealous, and I did feel a little used, I wanted that to backfire. If they felt better than me, I wanted them to feel less than me. Above all that, maybe even in a pathetic way, if I ever saw the dancing girl again, I wanted her to know that I wished that night she did not have to go. Maybe those things are true, or not, because in retrospect, the way I winked at her, with a grand sort of magnanimity, accomplished all of them. At the time, it just seemed the thing to do.

An odd ending. Perhaps banal. How hypnotized was I? That for days all I could think was of The Dancing Girl. How much would I love to dance with her again. Or even just to see her dance again. It really was quite amazing. I watch for her in the streets of the city. I always scan the dance floors. Just a chance to touch that magic. To re-open those closed doors. Or find that genie in a bottle. But in New York, you never see a body twice. I seek the dancing girl with open eyes. The odds-on bet must be I'll never find her. But, oh, to dance with Dancing Girl again. How hypnotized was I.

CHAPTER 4

EVE AND ADAM sat across from each other at an old, pit-ted, stone table. There was so much to talk about. So much to be curious about, and to wonder at. Although they spoke only for a little while.

"But, Atlantis is a faerie city, it's a legend in York!" Adam exclaimed excitedly, boyishly prey to his own enthusiasm.

Eve laughed, tried to suppress the laugh, then laughed harder.

"What?"

She laughed more.

"What, because I mentioned faeries again?"

"No, no, it's not that," she said chokingly, still giggling. A tear streamed down here face.

Adam glanced about himself in exasperation, as if appealing to imaginary spectators. Eve continued laughing, then slowed, looked at him, laughed more, and Adam's face turned red.

"It's just that – you talk funny," Eve finally said, bursting into laughter again.

"*I* talk funny?" Adam wondered incredulously, but was sucked into the humor of the moment.

The two of them sat at the table, laughing, gasping for breath, then laughing again. It was not entirely clear, even to themselves, what was so very funny, but for the first time these two young strangers, from two very different and far away places, felt completely comfortable with each other.

Still gasping for breath, Adam leaned forward and

touched Eve's hand affectionately. She drew back, startled, as if she had been struck. Which startled Adam, who turned pale. Eve looked at him accusingly, tensely, almost in shock.

"…You're the one who talks funny," he said finally. And, after one brief, tortured moment trying to suppress it, Eve burst into laughter again.

Adam ran his finger along a crack in the stone table top. He stole a momentary glance at her fingers and tried to seal in his mind how it had felt to hold them. Eve was looking down, her body drawn back away from him, trying to catch her breath. Wisps of hair hung attractively around her face, and she kept brushing them futilely aside, in a kind of scratching motion. She looked up again, and seemed to stare through Adam, with hard, penetrating eyes.

"But Atlantis—" he continued, looking at the ruined city around him. Ancient bricks overcome with moss and ivy. Encroaching forest that must have once been tamed. Long past forgotten, overgrowing fields. Noting, for the first time, the absence of walls. Or perhaps the forest was the wall.

"Atlantis is just a city. That's where I'm from," Eve said.

"It's not a faerie city?"

"It's not."

"No? Where is it?"

"Only a day or two from here," she said, then added, "if you walk fast, and if you know how to get there. Which I do."

The two young people stared motionlessly at each other. Trying to glean something – who was this being they were communicating with? What were they about? Where did they come from? What did they want? Learning nothing, but raising more questions than before.

"I'll have to be going soon," Adam said, "I'm late to start work on my garden. I must start planting and try to catch up with the others. And I don't even know if this plot that I'm looking for will work."

He was pointing to his map, but Eve did not understand him. She decided not to ask any more questions.

"Myself as well, I've quite a lot of work to do," she said.

"Well," Adam said, getting up, "God speed you on your journey then."

"And God speed you, sir," Eve said heartily. "And thank you again for the apple."

"It's nothing."

Adam walked to his bags and heaved them onto his shoulders, then pulled the heavy shovel from out of the ground and held it up like a walking stick. He turned back around to see Eve already walking limberly away, beautifully silhouetted on the crest of a small grassy rise. He started to say something, thought better of it, started again, stopped, turned around and marched heavily back toward the river.

"Adam!" Eve called out.

He turned around.

"Adam! I – I come back here sometimes. I can't say when, exactly, but I come here sometimes. Maybe I'll see you again. Here…" her voice trailed off, but she smiled at him.

"I look forward to it!" he rejoined.

Eve hesitated. Then ran down the hill and disappeared behind the rise. Adam could hear her footsteps trailing away. He turned around in a full circle, tracing the outlines of the city with his mind. Picked up an ancient cobblestone from off the ground and tossed it casually away. Then began to march. When he got to the river, he wondered if

this had all been a dream: the ruins, the girl, even the leopard. Or a vision. The great ancient city evaporated into
thick, fleshy forest and was gone, now only a vivid memory
and new mark on Adam's map.

Musically speaking this is more like a quick arpeggio than a piece. Literarily speaking it's more like a page or two torn out of somebody's scrapbook. Don't get your hopes up too high. Adam and Eve will be back directly.

I'M WALKING DOWN 5th Avenue and in front of me is this stunning blonde. She's about my age, wearing heels, a skirt, a tank top, with a cute little sweater in hand – not too dressed up, but not cheap looking; put together. It's 5 a.m. and she's heading towards the door of an apartment building. I just walk along behind her. To be honest, I was admiring the view.

Suddenly she turns and looks around. Eye contact. I'm a little shocked, but more so when, spinning on her heel, she walks over to me holding out her hand. "Hi, I'm Kelly, what's your name?" she says, a little too loudly. I'm probably lucky I wasn't drunk. Well, I shake her hand and we introduce ourselves.

"How are you doing tonight, Justin?" she asks in an intentionally sultry voice, and her eyes aren't quite right.

"I'm doing alright, how are you doing?"

"Absolutely wonderful, Justin," placing special emphasis on my name, as if breathless to utter it.

I don't stop walking, and she walks with me, stride for stride. We make small talk as we pass in front of my law school. Suddenly, she leans in close to me, her mouth almost touching my ear, "Do you like whispering, *Justin*?"

Really? I should probably eject from this conversation, but I have to see where it is going. Can't resist. I mean, don't get me wrong, I'm sure as hell not going to bed with a prostitute.

I keep my stride but kind of turn towards her, without leaning in, glance quizzically at her and make a "so-so" motion with my hand.

"It's ok," I say.

She screams startlingly, and with volume, "Hahaha, I *love* whispering, Justin!"

It's 5 a.m., the city is dead. I'm sure the screaming can be heard from a long ways off. I walk a little faster. Ten or fifteen yards in front of us a drunk middle-aged couple glances back and laughs.

Kelly's eyes bounce disturbingly around her skull as she enunciates another question, "Do you like Santa Claus, Justin?"

Um... Santa Claus? My perverse sense of humor gets the best of me, as I comment, "Santa Clause is awesome."

SMACK! She slaps me on the arm *as hard as she possibly can.* I'm not hurt, probably bruised, but it is a sudden, shocking, physically violent act. I hold my composure in check, betraying no reaction, and look her skeptically in the eyes as I start walking even faster.

At the top of her voice now, "*I LOVE SANTA CLAUSE, JUSTIN!!!!!*"

Kelly stops walking and starts spinning around in circles, screaming and laughing. I don't pause but only glance backwards as I continue on. The middle-aged couple in front of us have entered the lobby of a very expensive apartment building on 5th Avenue. Before the door closes, Kelly walks in quickly behind them, as if they are all together.

"Goodbye, Justin," she calls as the door swings shut and my feet carry me further away. I round the corner and am soon in front of my own building. It's about 5 a.m.

Your guess is as good as mine.

CHAPTER 5

ADAM FOLLOWED A white, winding river until it reached the broad lake he had seen from his tower. Blue water sought to outshine the sky, deep, and still. He wished he could sit down here and watch for hours. Glinting sunlight punctuated the lake's mirrored surface as long, silvery fish splashed out of the water and into it again. Adam stood on the bank trying to spot what kind of fish they were. Different from any he had ever seen before.

Using his map, it should now have been an elementary task for Adam to find the location of the old garden. It was marked clearly, as were nearby locating landmarks, great boulders and hills. But, though he searched diligently, he could not find it. The first day grew purple, grey, then dark, and another dawned more quickly than before.

As he circled the blue lake a second time, Adam thought aloud:

"Maybe he recorded the map wrong, maybe the garden isn't here at all!"

He skipped a stone across the unblemished surface of the water, it bounced 17 times before a silvery flash leapt up and swallowed it. He was already looking away.

"Could it be there never was a garden? Could it be the elder told me something that wasn't real? But that doesn't happen, and why would he do that? ...Why would mother and father tell me that Atlantis is a faerie city if it wasn't so?"

He marched back into the woods, plunging through great, aromatic ferns that ringed the lake. He rested his hand against an enormous tree, as if in affection, and leaned against it to rest his back. He continued through the forest more quickly, and spoke faster.

"But we were told that faeries will trick a person, that faeries are never honest. And if I've been talking to a faerie, she would tell me that Atlantis was not a faerie city, even if it was. But, she didn't look like a faerie, didn't act like a faerie, however a faerie may look. She was, like a girl. Different, but, like a girl."

High overhead, moving sinuously through the canopy of branches, two bright enormous eyes stared down at him. If you could float there, high, you could look into them and ponder what was inside. If you could get close enough, you could hear a heart, beating, quickening with the rise in Adam's voice. Perhaps if you were God you could feel the shallow breath across flared nostrils, or the resonant vibrations echoing in carefully pitched ears.

"What of Eve? Is there an Eve?" Adam continued obliviously, working himself into a rapture. "Could a girl be so beautiful, and so sweet, and, and... amazing? I have to say amazing. Do you hear that little bird, you trees and wild beasts, could a woman be so amazing? Surely a faerie, or a forest sprite, but a human girl?

"She was a match for me, you know! My equal, but, different... strong, and so feminine. Soft. You saw her look me in the eye, you trees!"

He gesticulated wildly to the sky with his arms, intoxicatingly free in that great open wilderness with no eyes to fall upon him. Free from himself. To himself.

"From Atlantis? Ha! Impossible! God grant I marry an Atlantean woman!"

Were it not for his shouting, Adam might have heard the movement overhead. Following. The slinking through the trees' thick canopy. He might have thought he saw a legendary creature once again. Thought.

He continued his stubborn search for the old garden, the prospect of starting his own, fresh from scratch, more appealing all the time. Wasn't that what his grandfather had recommended? What he would have done if he had not been given this map. Perhaps what he should have done anyway.

The map. It had not taken him where it said it would, and he had already lost a week's work. On the other hand, he had met Eve. Perhaps it evened out. He set off from the lakeshore again, towards a rock formation that was one of his map's landmarks, but turning away from it, on the right, where the map indicated to the left.

The eyes still followed him, from a distance. Evaluating, spying. They floated on the forest floor now. Walking. Traversing effortlessly, as born to it. A fly landed on Adam's face, and he brushed it away angrily, mortality catching up to his buoyant spirit. Hunger creeping up on him, pain and weariness. Eve wearing off of his mind, yet staying, somewhere in the back, churning and mixing with what was there before, fermenting into ideas that were new and different, that, when he finally started to catch hold of them, he could not quite describe. Disappearing now, amid more obvious, ephemeral things.

Adam recalled that he was running out of food, his bag of mana growing light. Running one week late, he had not yet begun the work to produce sustenance. After a week of nothing else, the taste of mana had grown very dull.

He marched to the edge of a small clearing and scanned it warily before sitting down at the base of a large tree along its edge. Shying from the unprotected open, granting the wilderness more caution now. He took out his last loaf of mana and began the late afternoon meal.

A shadow shifted across the clearing. At the edge of Adam's vision, flicker on the outskirts of reality. He froze, staring hard. Something was there, moving. Across the clearing, just inside the woods. Coming closer, watching him, moving forwards.

"H—"

"Hello there!" Eve shouted, materializing into open space between the trees. "Adam? Is that you?"

"H-h- Eve?" Adam stammered in amazement. "Eve! Hi. What are you doing here? H-how are you?"

They watched each other as Eve strode across the little clearing. Adam stood up. Nervous, happy, surprised. Confused as well. He wasn't sure why.

"I can't believe I ran into you again!" Eve said as she came closer, smiling a little too easily.

"Well... yeah. Wow. Come, sit down and eat with me," Adam said.

He bent forward hesitantly to kiss her cheek, but Eve drew back at the same instant, perhaps accidentally, and their feet shifted on the ground as each tried to find the comfortable distance to stand.

"Ok," Eve said, sitting down against a tree beside the one where Adam had been.

Adam sat back down, breaking off half of his loaf of mana and handing it to her.

"It's not much, I'm afraid," he said sheepishly.

"No more apples?"

"No more apples. No more left."

"What is this?"

Eve appraised the mana in her hand, breaking off a piece and examining it's peculiar texture. She rubbed a bit of it between her fingers and let it crumble to the ground.

"What's what?"

"This… food."

"What, the mana?"

"It's called 'mana'?"

"You don't know what mana is?!" Adam exclaimed.

"Should I know what it is?" Eve looked at him skeptically.

"No… No, I guess not, sorry. This food is called 'mana'. It's the fruit of God. It's the main thing we eat where I come from."

"Where does the mana come from?"

"Where does the mana come from? It doesn't come from anywhere. It's the fruit of God, it's just there."

"Hmmm…" Eve nibbled at the mana. "It's alright."

"What do you eat in Atlantis?" Adam asked.

Eve shrugged her shoulders.

"Lots of different things. Dried meat, corn, wheat. Bread, you know? Fruit when it's in season—"

"You eat meat? Animals?"

His eyes grew huge with horror.

"Yes. You don't?"

"No we don't! That's disgusting. Animals are sacred in York, we would never eat meat."

"Well you have a word for it," Eve said.

"That's true. I don't know why. I've never heard of someone eating meat. I don't even know how I know what it is."

Adam paused. Eve watched him unflinchingly.

"Is that strange, not to know how I know?"

He looked into her eyes, scanned her face. Hoping for some confirmation of himself. Scanning for the meanness of a being who would consume flesh, but finding only femininity and sweetness. Defeated by it, glancing down.

"I don't know," Eve said lightly, turning to stare out into

the clearing, as if it were nothing.

"You really eat meat?" Adam said again.

"I don't eat any meat except fish," Eve said. "My family are vegetarians. People in Atlantis eat meat."

"Oh, fish, well fish aren't animals," Adam said, with a note of relief in his voice. "That's not so bad. I knew you wouldn't."

"Well I have before. I just don't eat it now. It's not so bad you know. You think when you eat a plant that it wasn't alive, or when you pull a weed out of the ground?"

This new thought left Adam speechless.

"Life consumes life," Eve concluded simply.

She reached into her bag and withdrew two small, dry, sprouted plants, grinding them between her fingers and letting the crumbs fall onto the mana in her hand, then bit into it again, more hopefully.

"Mmmm, much better," Eve mumbled. "Here, try this."

Adam eyed her outstretched hand.

"They're just herbs," Eve said with exasperation, "that's what I collect in the forest. Plants, and nuts, and berries to take back and sell at the market in Atlantis. They're delicacies. Very rare."

Still unconvinced, Adam started to object.

"Here, give me your mana," Eve interrupted him, "I'll just put a little bit on it for you to try."

Reluctantly, he handed her the half.

"You're so suspicious," Eve said, scolding. She ground and sprinkled more of the small, dry plants and handed the mana back to him.

Adam thanked her with transparent insincerity, then forced himself to take a bite of the freshly seasoned mana which seemed to him freshly befouled. It was good! Pleasant new sensations awoke within his mouth. He thanked

Eve again, enthusiastically.

They ate and talked like the young people that they were, finding joy in this strange company where they had expected to be alone. Thrilling each other with exotic tales, easy and so mundane. After a while their voices did not seem strange to each other anymore, nor their mutual presence in the forest. Although the existence of civilizations other than York still loomed an enormous, impregnable quandary in Adam's mind.

"What do you see when you look into the forest?" Eve asked as they sat looking across the clearing, backs resting against the ancient trees.

"I see... trees, birds, ferns, earth, squirrels," Adam offered cooperatively, "I saw a leopard once. Is that what you mean?"

Eve stared in silence, gazing upon the forest as though it contained a hidden mystery, some inscrutable something that would eventually reveal itself to an exquisitely discerning mind.

"What do you see, Eve?"

"I see... Life. God. Sometimes my mother. I see something bigger than myself, something separate from me, but something I'm a part of. Sometimes I see money."

She paused. Adam sat very still, watching her, hardly drawing breath. She looked at him with an expression of vulnerability, even regret, and her voice quavered.

"Sometimes I think I see my home. Is that strange?"

"No," he said softly, "I don't think so. Maybe you just think about it more than most people. I see what you mean, though. Let me try again."

"Yes."

"I see rich earth," Adam said, "gardens, God's bounty waiting to be reaped. I see food sustaining thousands of faces back in York, beautiful, rich food to supplement the mana. I see the paintings of God, sometimes, in the bloom of a flower or the set of a tree. Once I saw His anger. And I see creatures, a multitude of creatures, amazing, wondrous things so much like us and yet so different. And I wonder what the difference is and I find no answers, but there it is, and I wonder what it means. I see strong men laboring in solitude through the fertile months, and I see them returning home, bearing the fruits of the harvest. I see all the smiling faces, and the feasts and celebrations."

"You see beautiful things," Eve said, blinking watery eyes.

"So do you."

Adam was suddenly uncomfortable. He began a slow process of standing up.

"You still never told me what you are doing out here," he said. "I thought you didn't come out this far."

"Oh? I do sometimes, just not often."

He bent to lift his heavy pack, and winced as the wound across his chest tore slightly open. He held his breath a moment, propping a hand against the tree.

"But, you're hurt!" Eve exclaimed, leaping up and reaching to touch him. "Let me see it."

"It's nothing. I'm alright."

Adam tried to twist politely out of her reach.

"You're not alright. Let me see it," Eve continued insistently, pulling at his rough, loosely fastened shirt. Adam hesitated, then unfastened a button to reveal the ugly, awkwardly wrapped wound underneath.

"My God, it's much worse than it looked before," Eve said, eyeing the black, weeping, loosely concealed flesh. She ran two fingers gently in a circle around its edges. "How can you walk around like that? Sit back down, let me tend to it."

Adam picked up her hand, not unaffectionately, and pushed her ever so gently away. She jerked angrily out of his grasp and stepped back close to him, pushing down and back on his forearms to move him against the tree. As he reached to nudge her back again she caught hold of his hand and twisted it quickly away, forcing him off balance, then took a step backwards, pulled herself up to her full height, almost on tiptoes, and glared.

"Sit down!" Eve ordered commandingly. As if she were an Empress, or some powerful princess. "I've quite a lot of experience with these sorts of things and that is a very dangerous injury. I'm not about to have you running around dying in *my* forest. In fact, I'm rather fond of you right now, and I'm not going to have you running around dying at all! Now sit down and let me tend to your wounded chest, as you've obviously no other woman around to do it for you, and are even more obviously unfit to do it yourself!"

Adam sat down in bewilderment. In a moment, he recovered his composure, and found himself inspired with a degree of self-satisfaction.

"Are you really rather fond of me right now?" he enquired, eyeing Eve rakishly as she examined his wound.

"Shut up."

Some of the herbs and plants Eve collected in the forest had medicinal properties. She fashioned them into a poultice, and removed Adam's makeshift wrap. Resting one small hand above the wound, she pressed the other softly against it, testing for tenderness. Four dark, septic looking gashes. Her eyes noted the smaller cuts and abrasions, mostly healed, that still peppered Adam's abdomen.

"What did this?"

"The leopard," Adam said simply. Then, in defense, "It

was attacking me before I even saw it."

"You really saw a leopard?"

"Yes, I told you that when I was telling you the things I see in the forest."

"I thought you meant you'd imagined it," Eve said, knitting her brow. "I always thought leopards were just mythological creatures, like chimeras, or faeries."

"That's what I thought, too. Imagine my surprise when I turned around and the monster was suddenly on top of me."

"You fought with it?"

Adam nodded.

"And you lived?"

"I'm more than a match for a leopard, you know," he said, and winked perversely.

"I've never heard of a leopard in these woods before. Is it dead?"

"I don't know," he admitted. "I hurt it, but it ran away into the woods. Maybe it died there."

"Wow," Eve said, at a loss for words.

"So," she continued thoughtfully, "first you saw a leopard. And then, later, you saw me. And you thought I was a faerie, because if leopard's are real, then faeries probably are too—"

"Something like that, yeah."

Adam picked at the half finished poultice, and Eve pushed his hand away. He smiled.

"You're starting to make sense to me, Adam," she said, and went back to work on his wound.

He sat tensely, in silence, enjoying the sensation of Eve so close beside him. The brush of her hands against his skin. Afraid that he would blink and she would disappear.

"What did you mean when you said that the wound on

my chest looked worse than before?" he asked abruptly.

"What?"

Eve's cheeks quivered.

"When you saw my chest, you said 'it looks worse than it did before'. But that's a strange thing to say. You never saw it before."

"Well," Eve bit her lip, but seemed almost to enjoy this turn in the conversation, "I was following you through the forest. I saw you rinse your chest off in a stream."

"You were following me? For how long?"

"Since we met."

"Since we met!" Adam said sharply, more befuddled than angry. "Since we met? Where did you sleep last night?"

"In the trees," Eve's eyes sparkled mischievously, "right above your head."

"In the trees," Adam sat up straight, sending bits of poultice and wrap cascading off his chest, serious now. "Wait. Wait, *why* were you following me?"

Eve stammered, somehow caught off guard by the obvious question.

"I don't know," she said, "I just, I didn't feel comfortable with a strange man wandering around in my forest. I had to see what you were up to."

"You *are* a faerie, aren't you!"

Eve burst into pleasant laughter, and Adam leaned back down against the tree.

"No, I'm really not. Now let me finish wrapping you up so we can both continue on our way."

She cleaned the wound with fresh water and with oil squeezed from one of her plants. The oil burned, but Eve worked quickly, ignoring occasional winces of pain that escaped Adam's fragile mask of composure. After the oil, Eve applied the poultice she had made, which had an immediate, mildly narcotic, cooling effect. She produced a spare, clean bolt of cloth from seemingly out of nowhere, and began tearing it into long, thin strips, laying them across Adam's chest.

"That's really a waste," he said stoically, "really, it's not necessary at all. You've done more than enough already. I'll be fine."

Eve continued tearing the cloth, ignoring him, and Adam gradually became aware of a burning sensation. Each time her skin touched his. Almost painful, but… pleasant. More than pleasant. His awareness made the sensation more intense, until it completely extinguished the pain of his wound. He stared into Eve's eyes again, finding only an impassive focus. Then she looked at him sharply.

"Lean up."

Adam leaned forward, and, as Eve stretched to wrap the bandages around him, something extraordinary happened. Her temple touched against his cheek. He felt it burn. The most wonderful burning. He caught his breath. Eve froze, still. Not drawing back. Knelt beside him, leaned over him, touching his cheek. Still. A frozen, euphoric moment. A small eternity, trapped out of time. No longer two people, but a single marble statue carved in stony white ambivalence to the world.

Adam turned his head and kissed her face where it had touched him. Eve leaned down, quickly, and kissed his collar bone, then fished the strip of cloth from behind his back and leaned away from him to tie it, once again the clinical, efficient nurse.

"There," she said, looping up the final knot, pulling the wrap as tight as it would go and drawing a gasp. "Just one last knot and, *there*. Now don't touch it for at least a week."

She stood, resting her hands on her hips and stretching

out her back. He stared up at her, and wondered what to do next.

They walked, after that, through the forest, and looked for Adam's garden. Talked, but not about each other. Avoiding a well that suddenly ran so deep, yet so remote, impossible. Giving no utterance to the gulf that ran between them, the walls that each would rather not describe. Eve taught Adam to find sustenance in this distant chamber of wilderness. Edible plants, and nuts, and parts of trees. Too quickly she had gone as far as she could go. Eve slowed to a stop and began to turn around, even to walk away.

"Do you have to go?" Adam wondered, knowing the answer.

"I have to go back to my home. To Atlantis. I'm already a day late, they'll be wondering what's happened to me soon."

"Well, I'm glad to have met you, Eve," Adam offered. Insufficiently, not knowing what else to say.

"I'm glad to have met you, too, Adam."

"I hope we will cross paths in the forest again."

"I do too. Goodbye!"

She melted into the forest and was gone. After a moment, Adam charged after her, but found only empty space between the trees, surrounding him on every side.

Free Jazz

This was more of an experimental
piece, does it fit in?

I mean, not so much in form, but more in content. Or maybe just it was an experimental night. Not exactly unprecedented. I mean, crazier things have happened to people, but... Like, what I'm trying to say is it doesn't exactly fit with all the rest, exactly, but it's related and kind of complements the whole. Or maybe it fits in, I dunno, you tell me.

I MET UP WITH my friend John and his roommate, Abe, and we headed to a party in Brooklyn. Saturday night. We hung out there for a little while. There were too many people we knew. People we had to be around every day who weren't necessarily our friends. I wonder if they felt the same. I mean, some of them, sure.

I ended up just kind of standing around by myself. Abe walked over surreptitiously and stood next to me.

"So," with an air of conspiracy, "John and I are leaving to go check out another party he knows about. Do you want to come?"

"Sure," I said, "what's the party?"

"Well, some girl who works at John's gym invited him to it. I don't really know much, but let's go, like, now, and John can tell you about it on the way."

I said goodbye to a few people and went downstairs. Fresh air – it felt good on my face, in my lungs. As fresh air is wont to do, I suppose. When you step out from some stale, cloying atmosphere or other, and into clean, cool, fresh air, it always seems a revelation. The same revelation again and again. Ever as sweet. Erm, anyways... I was outside for a few minutes before John and Abe caught up with me.

"Come on, let's go to the subway," John said, walking quickly, disinviting conversation until out of earshot of any possible other acquaintances.

Details emerged vaguely, reluctantly. There was something there, some something, a juicy potentiality, that John was hesitant to jinx through utterance. He would only reveal: 1) there was a party in midtown; 2) he had been invited by a trainer who worked at his gym; 3) she was hot; 4) there would be many female trainers there; 5) free liquor.

Which seemed pretty good, but didn't quite explain how hopped up and anxious my two friends were. There was something else, but I couldn't squeeze it out of them. Maybe they weren't even sure what it was themselves.

It was already midnight. We stood for a few minutes on a lonely subway platform in Brooklyn, waiting for the train back into the city. I was the tallest of the group, dressed lightly for the weather in a hooded sweatshirt, jeans, and sneakers. John and his roommate, in conspicuously expensive leather jackets and designer shoes, joked that I provided the 'street cred' for the group. I did enjoy the odd intimidating glower at other subway passengers along the way, but if they looked too uncomfortable I would smile.

We got to our stop and debated what street to try first (it turned out we didn't have an address, so much as a vaguely remembered description of the building), finally concluding that it didn't matter, and choosing the nearest street, which was 30th. After walking up and down 30th St. a couple of times we found the building we were looking for. There was no one out front, but we could hear music coming from up above. We pushed open the unbolted doors and walked in. People lay on the stairs in the entranceway, smoking.

"This Jeff's party?"

"Upstairs."

"Ok, thanks."

After a few flights of stairs in what seemed for all the world like an apartment building, we ran into a large open door, and a bouncer.

"Yeah?"

"Uh, we're here for Jeff's party."

"Go on in. Drinks at the back."

"Thanks, man."

We strode quickly through the door. In these types of situations you just don't ask questions. Not at first. At first you have to scope the scene. Get your bearings, pick up the rhythm of the place. Then you find the right people at the right moment, and then, if it's still not clear, you can find out what the hell is going on.

Inside, hip hop music thumped through a series of crowded rooms. A sweet, very hard faced woman shouted at us and smiled from a kind of coat check room. We gave her our coats and made our way slowly down a hall that connected all the rooms together. I'm not going to lie, I was pretty much just scanning the crowd checking out the women. Single minded. John and Abe were more immediately focused on liquor, I think. We soon had drinks, and it wasn't rotgut.

The place was a bit weird. It was hard to say exactly why. There were a series of rooms connected by a long, wide hall, with a large, couch-lined main room at the end. Here, in the crowded main room, a DJ was spinning some vinyl (all hip hop), a makeshift, open bar was jammed into the corner, rapidly serving up drinks, and 200 odd people danced, relaxed, stood around, or mingled. Plastic plants featured heavily in the decor, plush furniture, weird lights on the walls. Everything looked like it was here in the first place, not like it had been set-up for this particular party. It was sort of like a night club, and sort of like an apartment, but there was no cashier, no kitchen, no living area, no genuine bar, or — whatever it seemed like, it lacked the necessary content to be.

The crowd was peculiar, too. Mainly because an unusual number of massive men were standing around watching everyone. Rough, hard-looking, poorly dressed fellows all over 6'3" and weighing more than 300lb. They looked like bouncers, but not like they were working here, like they were also guests of the party. But, sort of like they weren't quite off the job, though. Had their eyes peeled wide for trouble. If that makes sense.

It turned out we were the only white people there. No Hispanics or Asians, either. All black. I felt pretty fucking cool because of that. Me, the brave, unbounded, unprejudiced center of attention. Not in a patronizing way, but in the way you feel when you get a foot in the door. It wasn't just the racial make-up of the audience, it was the whole scene, the whole weird atmosphere of the place. This wasn't Kansas anymore, you know what I mean? I could see that John and Abe were feeling the same. People stared at us, but not in an unfriendly way, and we began to mix in the crowd a little.

The social scene was hard to mix into, though. Everyone seemed to know their own crowd already, and John couldn't find the girl who had invited him to the party. Jackie. She would have been our in. We slowly circled through the people and enjoyed the atmosphere. Pounding music, dancing, screams, groups of women and men chatting loudly, quietly, laughing and whatever. There were a lot of chiseled bodies, male and female both. The security guys stared conspicuously, but tried to enjoy the party a little bit at the same time. Something weird about it all. An ambience. It was difficult to put your finger on.

I went and found the bathroom. A guard at the bathroom door let me in when I got to the front of a short line. The facilities were clean, decent. I mean, it's not like they were wearing a uniform or displaying a weapon or anything, although they did seem to have some sort of dress code, sweaters and slacks. Old sweaters. But anyway, even here there was that strangeness to the place. Halfway between a bathroom that you would find in someone's home, and one you would find in an office building. Everything about it was too neat and tidy, like a bathroom on a movie set. Not "lived in". You imagined a camera mounted on the ceiling watching you, and looked up to make sure it wasn't there. It wasn't, but were those mounting brackets bolted to the ceiling? One couldn't quite get close enough to tell.

I exited the bathroom, and considered the floor plan again as I walked around. Each room was sort of complete, in and of itself, but linked by doors to all the rooms around it. Like a motel. The rooms were neatly furnished, but with odd touches, like a mesh curtain hung as a screen around one of the couches in the main room. It might not sound weird, but it was. Out of place.

I caught up with John and Abe, who were also exploring, in one of the quieter side rooms that was temporarily empty. It was a bedroom sized room, with two couches, some large plastic house plants, and a 13 inch tv monitor bracketed to the wall above the door.

I chatted distractedly with my two friends, but could not help continually glancing around the room.

"We stumbled into some shit here," Abe said. "This is, like, some underground shit."

I looked up at the tv monitor on the wall. Strange. It started to make sense.

"I feel like porn has been filmed here," Abe continued. "Like, here. In this room. On this couch."

I glanced down at the couch where I was sat, imagining little HIV bugs crawling across its surface. Weird tentacle things with tiny wings, snot, and cilliae. [sic]

"And what's with that video monitor on the wall?" John said.

"Maybe they watch it while they film it."

"Yeah, you know," I said, "I think this is a bordello."

"A what?" Abe asked.

"A bordello."

"What's that?"

"You know what a bordello is, man," John said.

"I don't know what it is," Abe insisted.

"You know," I said, trying to think of the technical expression for the thing, "a, a – like, a whorehouse, man."

"Oh."

We decided to explore the place further, to try to see what we could see. And to look for this girl, Jackie, who had invited John to the party in the first place.

A smiling young man was greeting people near the door. He was maybe 23 years old, maybe younger. Fit. Apparently, one of the many professional trainers at the party. People were wishing him happy birthday.

"This must be Jeff," John said, moving forward, "he's the one the party is for."

We introduced ourselves to Jeff, and he seemed like he had been anticipating it. He was genuinely happy to have us there, almost disproportionately so. He acted like we were the insiders with him, the cool kids.

"Jackie?" Jeff said the name with an easy familiarity, "I know man, I haven't seen her tonight either. Jackie's an old friend of mine, we used to work together over at Equinox on 12th St. She better show up sooner or later, I'm telling you."

He laughed gregariously and wondered if any of us needed fresh drinks.

"What *is* this place?" Abe interjected, in a tone of awe.

"What, like, what do you mean?"

"Is this a club?"

"Oh, *this* place!" Jeff exclaimed. "It's my Mom's business. Yeah, sort of a club. Businessmen like to come up here and relax sometimes if they're having a long day, you know, that sort of thing. For a birthday present she's letting me have the party here."

I would have just left that lie, but curiosity had the best of Abe.

"Like, that's cool, but what kind of club is it? Like, I mean, is it open to the public? Can I come by?"

"Naww, man, naww. It's a fetish club. You got to be, like, a member."

Abe didn't even let it go at that. Kept asking questions. Jeff became more serious, and told us again that his Mom ran a "fetish club" for rich businessmen. She was the woman we had seen at the coat check. Jeff seemed embarrassed by the questions. Not ashamed, not in the sense that he felt bad about what the real answer was. More like, embarrassed that he was not at liberty to give a plain answer, to be frank with us.

Jeff seemed so *normal*. Better than normal. Bright, well mannered, seemingly well adjusted. One would have thought he had lived a rich, gloriously sheltered life in a suburb somewhere. One would have thought he was an innocent man. Yet here was his mother, a hard, deleterious looking woman, old before her time. Operator of this mysterious "underground" facility. Here were we in the den of iniquity itself. And here was Jeff, as sweet, gracious, polished, and, in addition to that, normal (seeming?) an individual as one would want to meet. I didn't know what to make of it.

Jeff excused himself politely to greet some new guests, and we continued our exploration of the "fetish club". A steady trickle of people filed past the landing outside the door, moving up the stairs. We went to see what was happening up there.

The staircase, as you moved up off of the landing, branched into one wide section that led to a series of small rooms, and a second, narrow section to the side of it, which was roped off. A sign indicated that this narrow staircase led to the roof. An inebriated couple came down from the roof as we passed and stepped surreptitiously over the rope.

Abe, John, and I followed the main stairs, and stepped into a smallish, dank little room filled with smoke and old couches. Some of the bouncers and other employees sat up here relaxing. Were they working tonight, or just here because...? Heads glanced up at us with mild suspicion, but nobody seemed to mind our being there. We started up a conversation with a young mulatto looking kid, he must have been all of 18, who seemed in a chatty mood. John and Abe instigated most of the talk.

"Can we go up on the roof, man?"

"Yeah, I don't think they're letting anybody up there now—"

"Nobody can go on the roof!" an enormous bouncer said gruffly, without taking his eyes from the screen of a small tv showing football highlights.

The kid shrugged his shoulders at us. A distinct smell of marijuana wafted in from one of the little rooms in the back.

"This place is wild," Abe said, "what's it like here normally?"

"It is what it is, man," the kid said philosophically.

"You work here?"

"You might say that."

"Well do you?"

"Sometimes I work here, sometimes I just hang out, you know."

"What do you do?"

"What do you mean, like, jobs?"

"Yeah, when you're working here, what do you do?"

"You know, just different odd jobs and stuff like that. It's a good place to work."

"What kind of business is it?"

"Man, you ask a lot of questions."

"Heh, no worries, bro." [That was my contribution to the conversation.]

"It's not like we're cops or something, come on," Abe said. "I'm just, we're just white boys from the Village, man, we don't see this kind of place every day. It's cool."

Some of our half-listening audience laughed.

"Haha, yeah," the kid said, relaxing a little, "yeah, man, I just do my job, I don't ask any questions."

"Jeff told us this is a fetish club, that means hookers and shit, right?"

"Yeah, man, I guess so. I don't really know much about what people are doing here. I just open doors for people, file papers and shit, collect my money at the end of the week. Whatever anyone else is doing I don't know about it, and I don't want to know about it."

"Don't know nothing, don't see nothing, don't ask any questions. You sound like a defense attorney," John said jokingly.

"These two guys are law students," Abe said, "they should know what they're talking about."

"Haha, get out of here, man."

"It's true! Don't worry, we're just here to chill out, though. We don't care what you guys are doing. Actually..."

At this point, John and Abe tried to find someone to

buy marijuana off of, and I wandered back out onto the landing. I don't use drugs, and don't like to have anything to do with them. It was disappointing. If John and Abe got ahold of some weed and smoked out, they would be too boring to hang out with. I'd have to enjoy the rest of the party solo. I made a mental note to look more diligently for a cute girl to cavort with.

The "I just do my job and don't ask questions" kid hooked my buddies up with some drug dealer or other, but I'm not sure if they bought any weed or not. I think they ended up not being able to agree a price.

When they came back onto the landing, John paused meaningfully, then dodged up the stairs to the roof.

"Fuuucckkk that," he said, "I want some fresh air."

Abe started up the stairs too, as if he was already planning to. I followed them as quickly as I could, but with apprehension. There's an attitude peculiar to the Pacific Northwest, an, "I'm just going to do whatever the fuck I want anyway." It's a cultural thing. Maybe John and Abe had more of this than me. We were all from there. Maybe they just had more to drink. We could get into some trouble here if we didn't tread lightly. Abe and John didn't respect that. But, I was glad, because I really wanted to see the roof.

We stepped through a metal door into thin city air, and gazed directly up at the Empire State Building. You could literally almost reach out and touch it, yet it hung fantastically in the air above, just out of reach. I had forgotten how close we were. The Bordello actually fronted onto it. As if the skyscraper were simply a tall turret of the castle floor we were standing on, lit up and shining in the night. Outshining the city. No movie could ever capture it so well.

We just said, "Wow." I crisscrossed the roof again and again, staring upwards. It was like there was this beautiful, jaw dropping thing that you had seen pictures of in books and magazines, on television and in the movies, this incredible human artifact of legend, and suddenly, one day, just at random, it was delivered to your feet, right there just for you, and more beautiful, more awesome, more special than you ever could have realized, and it was yours. You owned it.

Like what it was.

The bordello's roof itself, was a plain, stony grey affair, with random pipes, chimneys, and exhaust vents. Your typical New York City building top.

"Right, I got to take a piss," John said, and squared up against a corner wall.

"Good idea," Abe agreed immediately, staking out an opposite corner for himself while audibly unzipping his pants.

Man, I needed to piss too, but this wasn't my style. Nor was it something I was prepared to try to explain away if one of those bouncers decided to come up and have a smoke.

"You guys, don't– " I started to say, but piss was already hitting the wall. "Shit."

They both laughed. I walked back inside, and rejoined the party downstairs. Anyway, it gave me a chance to delay anyone who might be coming up, so I was sort of looking out for my friends to keep them from getting into too much trouble. Or even just from having their asses thrown out in the street, which is really the worst that was likely to happen.

I settled into a big, empty couch in one corner of the main room and watched the people and let the music wash over me. Groups came and sat down, chatting and laughing, and went as easily. All cool. Relaxed with me, because I was relaxed with them. Friendly because I was, and because they were. Just being easy.

Abe and John came by to see what was happening, then wandered off in different directions.

A pretty, 20-something girl came and sat down close to me on the couch. I could guess, from her lean, immaculately toned physique, that she was one of Jeff's trainer friends. It proved to be the case. Her name was Lisa.

Lisa and I talked for a long time about nothing in particular. John and Abe came by again, and I introduced Lisa to them, and they said hello goodbye, because they were both calling it an evening. It was early yet, perhaps only 2:00 a.m. I was enjoying relaxing on the couch, and Lisa was a pleasant conversation partner, so I just stayed there. Watched. I wasn't about to leave early, I might miss the best part!

Maybe my whole life in New York was like that.

I wasn't attracted to Lisa. Hard to say exactly why. I just wasn't. She was too much for me, I gathered that right away. I was scrupulously careful to avoid any flirtatious or romantic chat, to avoid sending mixed signals. Some of her male friends glanced over and stared suspiciously at me, and I could see it was mostly out of genuine concern. I certainly didn't want to be playing or disappointing anyone, so I tried hard to put myself in that "just a friend" conversational zone which women love so much when it suits them.

Lisa told me about her baby boys, and I looked at some pictures she had in her wallet. They were cute kids, and I wondered what their mom was doing out at *this* party, this late at night. But I guess even single moms need breaks, too. Probably need them more than anyone. I didn't raise the point at all, but Lisa told me defensively about the multiple jobs she was working, the classes she was taking, and how hard she was trying to give her boys a good life. And how difficult it was.

I told her she can't have been going too far wrong if her babies were looking so healthy and happy.

We talked about hip hop, of which Lisa was a big fan, and I boasted that I mostly liked, "more hardcore style rap." When pressed about what groups, or performers in particular, I could name only Tupac and Biggie Smalls. Lisa quizzed me good naturedly about many underground groups I might have heard of [I hadn't], but changed the subject graciously when it became clear how limited my knowledge was.

Our conversation wasn't memorable, it was just pleasant. One of us eventually decided it was time for them to head home. I don't remember who, but it was.

We ran into each other again at the coat check. In the bright entranceway lights, Lisa looked different. Harder, more haunted, somehow more fragile. I squeezed her hand to wish her good night, and leaned forward to kiss her cheek, as the custom goes.

She leaned forward just then as well and our cheeks banged together with a disturbing crack. I apologized quickly. Lisa played it off as nothing, just smiled a friendly good night to me and waved as I retreated. But the force of the impact had literally made me dizzy. For her, being quite a bit smaller than myself, it must have been terribly painful. Or maybe she had more to drink than I realized, and wasn't feeling much of anything at all. Either way, I felt bad about it. She probably had been attracted to me, and I probably had hurt her pride already.

Jeff stood just inside the entrance off the stairs, embracing guests and wishing them well as they made their way back out into the night. He gripped my hand and clapped his arm around me like we were old friends, and thanked me again for coming by. I thanked him for being such a gracious host. Then I was down the stairs again, into the cold air.

It was about 4 a.m. as I walked home along 6th Avenue. New York has been called "the city that never sleeps", but it does. Between the hours of four and six it's actually pretty quiet. Not unlike the late nighttime, or early morning in most places. The streets are rather pleasant those hours. Peaceful. I walked the 25 blocks or so back home, as I was often wont to do. Thinking about Lisa, and Jeff, and John and Abe. Thinking about life. And not really understanding, but gaining something from the effort.

CHAPTER 6

THE NEXT MORNING, Adam found the overgrown garden he was looking for, improbably concealed behind a thick patch of small trees. The whole little area was hidden from view by foliage and terrain, and not quite where it had been marked out on the map. But it was certainly the place he had been looking for. To the eyes of a gardener it was immediately, viscerally, spectacular.

Fallow land emerged from behind the clustered trees and erupted in rich with life. Flat, long ago churned earth set out and apart from the woods. Enormous Yorkish crops, gone feral, now producing on their own. Dark, wet soil encroached upon by early blooming wildflowers, scattered here and there. Fresh water, brooks and streams. Adam scooped up a handful of the earth and brushed his lips across it, almost in a kiss, savoring the unmistakable nutrient scent, even tasting it.

His brain automatically measured the spaces and decided where different plants would go. The Yorkish plants still flourishing here, left over from their careful planting long ago, would catch him up on the time he had lost. With a garden plot such as this, almost inconceivably ideal, he scarce needed catching up. None of the other young tenders were likely to have found its equal, or even a plot of land that approached it.

Still, Adam was injured and not yet at his full strength. Still again, Adam was York's most promising young gardener. In any event, this was not a competition, as Adam knew. Though, in any event, he shouldered the burden of heavy expectations.

The words of his grandfather came back to him, "Make a garden of your own, Adam, make it your own. Don't follow anyone else's lead. Don't build on top of anyone else's work."

But what a plot this was! It easily exceeded Adam's high hopes. He proceeded through the fields, relishing the crunch of soft earth under his feet. He picked fruit and leaves, wild cultivated bounty, and prepared a proper meal. While he cooked and ate, he sketched out gardening plans in his head.

After finishing his meal, Adam picked up his hoe and walked to a weedy, fruitless patch of earth at the garden's edge. Lifting the tool energetically, high overhead, he prepared to churn and clear the ground. He shifted his weight expertly forward at the hips and moved to bring the hoe crashing down. But could not. An invisible force stopped his hand. The hoe sank slowly to the earth.

"Here now," Adam said to himself, and raised the heavy stone tool back into the air, "Hup!"

There was no thud of cutting, crunching earth. He could not. The tool hung quivering in the air.

An image of Eve appeared before him, unwelcome and unbid. Not as an apparition, not a part of reality, but in his mind's eye. It was as real to him as real, without the pretense of reality. She looked at him accusingly, beseeching. She laughed at him, then looked away, which was worse, and ignored him.

"Why don't you make a garden of your own?" Adam heard her say.

Then he felt a twinge of pain in his stomach. His skin crawled and he became feverish. The garden hoe quivered on the ends of Adam's clenched muscles, trapped in suspension, churning the air bizarrely until he collapsed to the ground in confusion and pain.

He lay there in the field, tormented. Gripped by emotion he could neither explain nor understand. Overcome by the inexplicable compulsion to leave this long abandoned place and never return. There was a place he was supposed to be, though he knew not where. Not here. The vision of Eve had subsided, but he could not push her from his thoughts. Or the words of advice from his grandfather. They wrapped together. Above them, more immediate and real, was simply the pain, the wrongness, and the sense that somewhere else was right.

Feverishly, Adam lifted his belongings into a great pile in his arms and stumbled back into the forest. He wandered through the woods unconsciously, lost in the storming emergence of - what? There were no words for it. Shadowy, insubstantial something. Ethereal mists of the universe become concrete. And acting upon him. Pain of a future being lost. Some vital, living organ – injured – an integral part of himself he had never guessed at.

As his footsteps carried him away, the pain gradually subsided, leaving Adam in solitude with the daze, and the mystery, and wonderment of it all.

Time passed. Adam stood on the outskirts of the ancient, abandoned city. Transported, as it were, by feet and paths unknown. He stumbled from the darkness of the forest, into an ancient, abandoned avenue, and wondered if it was real. If it ever had been real. Or how reality could fit his mood so easily.

How could he have been fooled by a faerie girl? Some trick of majik. Or how could he not?

Adam walked through the raggedly cobbled, ruined streets. The city was lit with crisp, white, full moon light. He walked to the wall where Eve had sat, and lay on it, and tried to remember exactly what she had looked like. He could only remember the sound of her voice, singing, and that she was beautiful.

Stars shone against the clear sky above the city, multicolored tapers lit in honor of the mummified remains. Adam climbed again to the top of his tall tower and painted the stars with his fingers, touching them, bonding himself to the heavens. He traced out the constellations taught to him by his father and grandfathers, imagining the old stories told around fires at night. The snake entwined in battle with Peter; the dragon; the ancient goddess of love, from the time before man knew God. He saw her clearly now, lit up magnificently. With brush strokes of his being, he poured her colors out across the sky.

Each constellation he painted in turn, and her again. Even then, in the deep stillness of the night, these rested on the surface of his mind. Insignificantly essential – there, but absent – conjured, in turn, and forgotten as quickly, skittering across still troubled waters and then gone. What remained, what sounded through them, was the haunting, sweet echo of Eve's song, mysteriously caught upon the air. How could it be? The night grew deep, and Adam finally still, listening to the echo unabashed. No longer trying to understand or control, but only to savor it.

He slept there, on top of the tower. Dreamed deeply things he could not later remember and woke early to rays of the dawning sun. Again Adam surveyed his horizon, examining the city more critically than before. It was a thing of brickwork; large, brown bricks and crumbling plaster. The bricks were stacked ingeniously, often in intricate patterns, forming row after uneven row of multistoried buildings. Three, or four, or even five floors high, with an occasional temple or tower rising up to dwarf the rest.

Glinting mysteriously in the sunlight, illuminated by the hand of God, were two flat swaths of land that encircled the east end of the city. Adam stared at them, transfixed. The sparkling seemed to mirror something in his mind. It looked unnatural. He climbed down from the tower and went to investigate, hoping to distract himself from the thought that Eve would be here again. Here, in this deserted city. He was overfilled with it.

Up close, the fields glistened with morning dew, but were not unusual. Rolling fields of wild grass. Every dozen feet or so, the faint outline of an ancient furrow bore witness to the fact that these fields had once been farmed.

He walked far out into the grass and surveyed an enormous farming plain. Larger than he had thought when viewing it from above. The grass was rich, healthy. Deep green, even now before the rains had begun. The ground, flat and even. Adam knelt and dug into the thick, fibrous root system, breaking through to the earth underneath. He kneaded it in his hands to test its texture, catching the dusty aroma off the air, taking the measure of its quality. Rich, unimpeachable earth. Not quite so rich, perhaps, as that of the map garden, or as well irrigated – not so magnificently virile. Yet, as good as any earth a man was likely to find.

"I could keep a fine home in one of these abandoned buildings," Adam mused to himself. "When Eve came back again, I would set a lovely table for her."

He walked back to the grass' edge and took the stone hoe in hand.

"Hup!" Adam lifted the heavy tool into the air and slammed it down through the roots of the grass. "Hup! Hup!" he swung again and again, turning the head neatly after each stroke, churning the earth.

He continued tirelessly through the day, and through the week, catching up work he had lost, preparing his fields. Late each afternoon, while there was yet light in the sky, he explored the abandoned city, contemplating those who built it and what had happened to them. He cleaned up a lonely, stunted tower near the fields, that he had chosen for his home.

In the evenings, Adam sat by the firelight thinking about the abandoned city, Atlantis, York, and Eve. Wondering what it all meant, and what it was he had never understood about the world. As he sat by the fire, his hands worked and worked away, carving green jade and black onyx stones pried from inlays on the disintegrating city walls. Shaping and polishing them into intricately patterned beads. Each finished bead he strung onto a narrow length of cord.

Adam sung quietly to himself as he carved the beads. Mostly songs from the fires at York, but sometimes a new song, one he knew only incompletely.

"In my life, in my life. In my life, in my life....."

faerie tale reading in female voice

And now for something completely the same...

"FAERIE TEARS INK"

Once upon a time,

In a little kingdom in Faerie Land, there lived a Little Boy with many gifts. And people loved him for the gifts he had. So things came easily to the Little Boy in Faerie Land. And the Little Boy was filled with natural goodness. He never took advantage of his gifts, although he knew they loved him for the gifts. And the little boy was the prince of lads, in Faerie Land.

Time passed, and the Little Boy grew older. The Little Boy grew up. And he had to leave Faerie Land, where everyone loved the special Little Boy. The Little Boy left Faerie Land, to make his way in The World.

"Fare thee well!" called the Little Boy, as he left his lovely Faerie Land. "I've a dream to find, out in The World. I've always dreamed of the Golden Bounty. Everyone in The World has found their Golden Bounty. But in Faerie Land there is no Golden Bounty."

"Fare you well, good Little Boy!" they called, "Give your wonderful gifts to The World, good Little Boy. Give your gifts to The World and find your Golden Bounty."

So the good Little Boy grew up and went out into The World. The World that was so different from Faerie Land. The good Little Boy could not have known how The World would be. But he believed in the Golden Bounty.

"Here are my gifts, World." said the Little Boy, "Here are my gifts, World, now where is my Golden Bounty?"

And The World looked at the Little Boy and laughed. A

mean laugh, the laughter of The World. "Your gifts are shit, Boy. How should We know where your Bounty is, Boy? Why would We give to you, Boy? Find your own Bounty yourself, Boy!"

All his life the Little Boy had one dream and one dream only: to go into The World and find his Golden Bounty. And it was true that people from The World all had a Bounty of their own. And Golden Bounties were a common thing. But the gifts of an innocent Faerie Boy mean nothing to The World. The World would never give a Faerie Boy his Golden Bounty. Though the World knew well where to find her.

All he wanted in The World was to find his Golden Bounty. The good Little Boy could never return to Faerie Land. The Little Boy of many gifts became an ordinary Lonely Man. "Why did they take my Golden Bounty?" thought The Boy.

But in Faerie Land they danced and cheered, happy and proud of the dream they believed their Little Boy had found in The World. And The World laughed again. And the Little Boy cried Faerie Tears.

CHAPTER 7

TWO WEEKS LATER, Adam stood near the end of a long row of tilled earth, stripped to the waist in the midday heat. In his left hand he carried a seed sack, already half empty. His back popped audibly as he stretched it out, briefly relieving the strain from hours hunched over planting seeds.

"She did say she would be back," he commented to himself, as a salty bead of sweat slipped down his forehead, along the ridge of his nose, and plunged from his body like a diver, only to splash onto his toes below.

Adam followed the humped up furrow of earth, pushing maize seeds down equidistantly, thumb deep, as he went. The ancient city glowed enigmatically in the bright landscape behind him.

"She said 'sometimes'," he continued, " 'sometimes', as if it were an invitation. But she's not here, she hasn't come back. Faerie girl. Could she have changed her mind? Perhaps she thought better and decided not to see me again. She could probably pass through here and I wouldn't see her. Or maybe she is always here, haunting this place. Revealing herself just long enough to trap you."

He glanced up at the patchwork beauty of the towering brick skyline behind him. The random patterns that somehow fit, and became more than they should have been: a thing to take your breath away.

"This city. What city? What city ever was there other than York. York was at the beginning of all creation, has been through all the ages, and who ever heard of anyplace else? Any real place. Not here, not on this earth."

Eve watched him from the edge of the field, smiling, concealed in the scrub brush. Pricking up her ears as hard as she could, catching his words only incompletely.

"Atlantis, ha! A child's tale! Five days from York you say? A week? And nobody has ever found it before? Ridiculous. How could I be such a fool.

"But who ever heard of a leopard? Or a real faerie. An ancient city on the river. Or a beautiful girl in the woods, that one could kiss?

He paused in his work and brought his hand to the healing scars across his chest.

"A girl in the woods to nurse your wounds, to heal you. Faerie? As much a girl as any I have known.

"Sometimes...

The sentence broke away.

"I remember she liked apples," he concluded to himself.

Eve sat quietly in the brush, enjoying watching Adam work. Enjoying watching the midday sun play across the muscles of his bare flesh. Knowing he was thinking of her, and that she loved him.

"Adam!" comes the happy shout from across the field.

His heart stops a moment and his stomach turns over as he glances up, then relaxes when he sees her face. The rightness of it. She steps neatly through the furrows, sensitive to the planting he has done. He runs to meet her, of course; he can't help himself.

They reach each other and stop. Smile. He leans forward to kiss her cheek and she reaches out to hug him. Then they reverse, then laugh. She offers her hand and he kneels down graciously to kiss it, which makes her blush. Then they are walking together, a bit aimlessly, and somebody has to speak.

"You've been working awfully hard, Adam."

"I always work hard," he replies innocently. "I was just thinking of you when you appeared."

"Were you?"

"Thinking you might not come back here. Eve, I'm awfully glad you did."

"Of course I would come back. Are you—" she pauses in mid-sentence and changes her mind, "it's a lovely garden, Adam."

"What, this? But nothing's even growing yet. Just wait."

Then he realizes that he said something wrong, or something not quite perfect, so he stops and looks into her eyes.

"Thank you," he says solemnly, and her lip twitches as they walk again.

"You should see the gardens outside York," he says, resuming the conversation.

"They must be awfully beautiful," she says. "Is it much like York here?"

"Well I'm here, and now there's a garden, and a lot of stones."

"Yes, I gathered that you Yorkers had a lot of stone."

"In York everything is stone."

"I can almost believe that."

They walk silently, and he reaches out and squeezes her hand. Then they reach the place he had been working and stop again. And stutter, finding almost too much to say. They both blush.

"Is Atlantis really only a day's walk from here?" he asks.

"A day or two if you hurry, and if you know how to get there."

"Next time you will come back sooner," he says commandingly, and she starts to be offended, but stops and giggles, accepting the play-ful expression on his face.

"We'll see."

He looks down at the work he has done and wonders if he can afford to stop for the day. She interrupts before he can decide.

"I didn't mean to interrupt your work—"

"Oh—"

"I mean, I've still a lot to do myself today. I just wanted to come and see if you were here."

"Um—"

"I'll leave you alone for now, Adam, it's just good to see you."

She starts to walk away.

"W-Wait! Stop. I've been waiting two weeks to see you again."

"I've been waiting to see you too," she says softly, almost in a whisper, and he wonders if he really heard it.

"Well, well, why don't you come back tonight and eat with me."

"Thank you, I'd like that."

"You'll come?"

"Yes. What will we be preparing?"

"...Fish."

"Then I will see you at sunset, Adam."

And she is jogging off towards the trees.

"Er, Eve. I'm staying in that tower," he says, pointing. "Over there!"

"Right!"

She floats across the field and disappears into the woods. He stands in the middle of it, alone again and silent — for a few minutes, dazed. Then shrugs his shoulders and resumes his work.

That afternoon, Adam stopped early and went to set his traps. He caught three catfish in the river, gutting them with his glass blade. He prepared a roaring fire in the tower hearth, and was just mixing together a bread of sorts, from ground up wild corn, when Eve arrived.

"Hello?" she said, peeking in through the tower door. "Oh, Adam, there you are."

"Eve! I'm just starting on the bread."

She crossed the broad main room to the hearth, looking over his work. The warm red heat of the fire mixed with gentle purple and rose hues of the setting sun outside, casting their faces aglow.

"Are you making bread? With what?"

"See, I've collected some wild corn and dried it in the sun. Then ground it. It's not bad."

"Three whole catfish, wow," Eve said, surveying the kitchen.

"It's not so much, on the one hand," Adam said evenly, "but on the other it's a real feast."

"Here, don't start cooking this yet," Eve said, "come out and watch the sunset with me. Then I will help you with the cooking."

Adam took her by the hand and they walked outside together, sitting down against the side of the tower, facing the sun. The sky was a wash of magentas, pinks, orange, and blue. Glowing, godlike clouds sparked with hints of condensation. Birds flew gracefully overhead. Song birds here, and in the distance a hawk – or a buzzard, it was hard to tell for sure.

"I often like to sit and watch the sunset," Eve said, leaning against Adam and resting her head on his shoulder. "Did you ever watch the sunset from the top of a tall tree?"

"I don't think so, no. I never have," Adam said, trying to remember times he had sat and watched the sunset before.

"Oh, you should. It's the best way to watch a sunset. Well, this is nice, too, but when you are in the top of a tall, tall tree – it's like, you're there. Among it. Among the colors of the sky. With the breeze, and the wind, and the clouds. The sun. And you. It's the most amazing feeling."

"I don't think I make it to the top of very many trees," Adam said, "but that sounds wonderful."

"Ah? That's my specialty, climbing trees. I'm the best at

it. That's why I'm so good at collecting delicacies in the forest."

"Is it?"

"Well, that's part of it. And I *am* the best."

Eve began to worry that she sounded too conceited, but was unsure how to temper Adam's impression of her.

"I love sunsets," she finally concluded, and squeezed his arm to her.

"I love you," Adam said sincerely.

They nestled together against the crumbling brick wall, watching the sunset, hardly noticing it. Their universe compacted to a single pinprick of experience, the feeling of their love leaning against themself, and the trying to appreciate it, to understand how it felt and what it meant.

"How can you say you love me, when for all you know I really am a faerie?" Eve said, kissing his cheek and snuggling up tighter against him.

"For all you know, I'm really a faerie prince."

"Oh ho!" and she giggled.

"I don't know, I just do. I just love you. I don't know why."

"I know. I know what you mean."

It was beginning to get dark, so they made their way into the tower to prepare dinner. The fire in the hearth was still high, the room hot but for breezes that blew up off the river and rushed inside through unobstructed windows.

Eve contributed some of her herbs and berries to their ingredients stock and soon they had prepared a feast. Or as good as a feast. Savory fish with fresh, crisp, aromatic bread. Mushrooms for a garnish, berries an appetizer. All sweetened with the brush of fingers together, touch of shoulder against arm; the gentle, semi-conscious affection of the preparation. It affected the flavor in such a profound way. The most effective sweetener of all.

Their meal passed far too quickly, at a little wooden table Adam had made, sitting on flat surfaced boulders he dragged in for chairs. Adam thought to bring up the subject of eating flesh again, so did Eve, but they each for their own part decided not to. Neither would do anything to mar the pleasure of the moment, the feeling of being together. Which made them reticent, but sort of gentle – secure. Mostly they talked about their day, and superficial details of the time they had spent apart. Simple things. How happy she was to find him still at the ruins. How happy he was that she had come back. How exciting it was to see each other again. How funny when they had met.

"Why did you decide to offer me an apple?" Eve wondered, smiling.

"You really do love apples."

"Well don't you?"

"I guess so. I do now," Adam said easily, a little bemused.

"Adam, in Atlantis apples are very rare."

"Are they?"

"Have you ever seen an apple tree growing in the forest?" she asked.

"...No, I guess not."

"There is one apple tree in Atlantis. One. It blooms in the courtyard of the Grand Palace. I saw it once when I was a little girl. It produces fewer than a dozen apples a year, and only the royal family are allowed to eat them."

"Really?" he wondered incredulously.

"Yes, really. Where did you get your apples?"

"I never thought about it before. There *are* no apple trees in the forest. How strange."

"Well where did you get yours, then?" Eve asked again,

insistently.

"Where? Well, in York there are groves and groves of them. Of apple trees. Lots of different kinds."

"You have more than one apple tree?" her eyes were huge.

"Not more than one, thousands of them. We eat apples almost as much as mana. It's very strange that they don't grow in the forest. It never occurred to me before."

"Thousands..."

"Thousands. Groves and groves. They grow in the streets, sometimes even on rooftops. To be honest, they can be a bit of a pest."

"A pest?"

"Don't misunderstand, apples are sacred in York. Sort of like mana."

"You're saying that just a few days from here-"

"Five or six."

"That five or six days journey from here, there lies a great, enormous stone city where magical bread appears from heaven, and that is filled with *groves* of apple trees?

"Yes...?"

"It's hard to believe," Eve said conclusively.

"Well, your stories are stranger than that!"

"How are my stories strange?"

"You come from *Atlantis*, a city that doesn't exist."

"It does exist."

"Groves of apple trees aren't hard to believe; only *one* apple tree that produces less than a dozen apples a year is hard to believe."

"Why? I saw it when I was a little girl. The apples are consumed every year at the climax of the royal apples feast."

"It must be an amazing place," they said simultaneously,

each trying to accept the truth in their heart: that the strange, sweet, beautiful person across the table really was who he or she pretended to be. Neither quite convinced.

"I'm getting tired, Adam. I had better go."

"Already?"

"Already."

"Well, well where will you go? Why don't you sleep here tonight," Adam offered innocently.

Eve laughed, hurting him without intending to. He wondered what was so funny.

"No. Thank you. I sleep in the trees."

"In the trees, how-"

"It was a lovely dinner, Adam. Thank you."

Eve embraced him tightly, stretched onto her tiptoes and kissed him warmly on both cheeks, but turned determinedly away from his lips. Then she walked quickly to the door.

"Wait!"

"Yes?"

"When will I see you again?"

"You'll see me. Maybe tomorrow. Goodbye, Adam."

She ran out the door and disappeared into the night.

Adam hurried to the window to witness Eve's escape, but spied only dreary darkness and bright star-night sky.

"Maybe," he repeated wistfully to himself.

That night Adam sat late by the fire, finishing work on the jade and onyx necklace. Imagining the life of a beautiful girl in a great city called Atlantis, who often wandered the woods by herself, and who had seen an apple tree, *once*, when she was a little girl.

Cadenza

Some Things Remembered

           This gets more to the heart of the thing. Perhaps it is the genesis of the whole damn book. I'm not sure. It's what I care the most about, and hopefully you will too. Or, if not -- well, I wouldn't say I failed exactly. Just see what you think.

As I walked Nathalie to the subway, I wondered when I would see her again.

"Yes, Justin, I don't know. Of course I want to see you again, but this is my last time in New York, so to say, and I have many people to see. I will try to call you tonight when I am in."

It hurt to hear this. Was hard on my heart. I put my hands around her waist and pulled Nathalie in against me, trying to read something in her eyes. Trying to confirm that what I was feeling was really shared. Terrified she would object, or pull away.

"Nathalie, it's me. You should make time for me."

"Yes, I know it's you," she said distantly, as if to a stranger. As if to say, "There's nothing here for you."

But I held onto her, unwavering. Still capturing her distant eyes, still looking for something. A silent second that seemed an eternity. And her eyes softened and she was looking at me again.

"Yes… I know," she said softly. "But I don't know what I can do."

"See me tomorrow. You can."

"Justin, I'll try. I really have to go."

Nathalie hugged me and walked away.

~   ~   ~

After finishing lunch, Nathalie and I walked the long way back to my apartment. Eking out each tiny drip of time. We would get back to my apartment, and she would have to go. It would be a hard goodbye. So we walked, and talked, and tried not to think about it. I couldn't help doing so.

A heart beat in time and we were in front of my building. It was never harder to walk through those doors. I had walked through them before while I was dying. Now every footstep sounded a death knell. Strangely harder than my own death. Yet, here, still, was the girl beside me. So bitter, and so so sweet. In the elevator we leaned our heads together, skull to skull. As if to reify our tenuous connection. In silence.

~ ~ ~

I leaned in close to Nathalie, and she leaned in to me. Stood close. She said sweet things about places she had been that you would think would be expensive but don't have to be and how I should go. I said she should come explore the Village with me. She thought so too. We tried to exchange numbers, but there were some issues with her cell phone. It was a Swiss phone. She gave me her number, though. And e-mail just in case.

Everyone wanted to leave now, but my brother held them off and made them leave me alone. Good man. Eventually, we really had to go. I wanted to leave on a high note anyway. Why wait until things get awkward, when you just met and feelings are powerful already? Why not pause and savor that, and give it room to grow?

I gave Nathalie my best European kisses on each cheek, and went downstairs with my friends. Stepped into the bathroom for a moment. People were getting impatient. As we walked to the door, Nathalie was sitting on the couch staring at me. Eyes huge like saucers. I looked back and

smiled instinctively. I think I wanted to leave before something went wrong.

~   ~   ~

The "No Malice Palace" was a little bar/club in the East
Village. About a month earlier it had been the first bar I
had ever gone into alone. It might have been the first bar I
had ever gone into at all, but I can't remember for sure. It
took courage for me to walk through the streets of New
York alone and step into a little club and make friends with
the strangers there. Everyone liked me. When I came to
New York, it was weird, it was like I had fallen backwards
into my element. Everyone wanted to embrace me. I hadn't
felt that way since I was a child.

For once in my life I didn't get lost. Maybe because I
wasn't thinking about it. Nathalie and I had walked at least a
mile, but it seemed like we got there instantly.

The Palace was foreboding on a dark wet night like this.
A blank wall with no sign, dim candlelight barely escaping
the window, and a black imposing steel door. For a moment
I thought it was closed.

With feigned confidence, I pulled open the door and
ushered Nathalie into the glow. Amber candlelight reflected
off the pressed tin ceiling, and our eyes slowly adjusted to
the dim. We were the only ones there, and the lone bartender was excited to have customers. He chatted with us a
moment and could not stop grinning at Nathalie, although
he seemed to be trying not to. She had that effect on men.
The bartender made us at home, though, and left us to our
own business. We settled down on a couch in the back and
ordered a couple of drinks. And talked and got close to

each other.

I held her hands and kissed them. I kissed her face. Pulled her in tight. And she leaned into me and cooed. Such a feminine creature.

But every time I leaned to kiss her lips, she turned them away and let me kiss another spot on her face. This didn't make any sense to me, and was making me nervous. In truth, I had never kissed a girl before, so it was particularly painful and strange. All her body language was embracing me, and her eyes were beautiful and swollen, yet she turned away.

"You don't want to kiss me?" I asked, confused.

"There is a problem," She said softly.

"What problem? Kiss me."

She turned her face away again, and I kissed her temple.

"Yes, you see, I have a boyfriend."

I didn't know what to do with that. I'm not a mercenary person, I can't be. It's just not in my nature. My immediate thought was not how to overcome her reticence, but whether I should even try. I don't want to mess up anyone's life or persuade them to do things they will regret.

"That's not fair," I whispered into her ear, and things continued as they had been, whispering to each other, pulling her tight to me and kissing her face – but never her lips. Her embracing me and then turning away at the last moment.

No one else showed up to the bar that night. We got the bartender to take a few pictures of us together. I love those pictures. I went downstairs a moment just before we left, and when I got back Nathalie had already paid our tab. I wanted to pick it up, or even just pay half, but she wouldn't let me.

~   ~   ~

"Are you religious?" I asked, trying to sound casual. Nathalie was almost startled by the question.

"What do you mean?"

"Like, back home in Switzerland, do you go to church? Are you a Christian?"

"Yes, yes, I am, so to say, Catholic, and I go to church with my family. And you?"

"Me too. I mean, I'm protestant, but I'm pretty religious. I think that's really cool. What do you think about the Catholic church?"

"Gosh, Justin, I don't know," she faltered, trying to figure out where I was going with this. She watched me closely, curiously.

"I just think it's really interesting. The Catholic church I mean – it seems very different from what I grew up with," I explained. "Like, what do you think about priests, and confessional, and all that stuff?"

Nathalie grew thoughtful for a moment. She seemed, in the end, a little bit charmed by this inquiry. That I really cared what her ideas were. That it was important to me.

"You know, being a priest, it is a hard life. They are really forced to be – apart from the rest of society. It is good, and admirable, but for the Church I think it is difficult, because they can't understand the life of normal people, so to say. They are separated, and they have to be alone, yes, so I think it is hard for them to know what the experiences of other people are like and understand them."

As Nathalie continued with her thoughts on the Catholic church, I didn't need to ask any more questions. To me, whenever I was with her, Nathalie was perfect. It was wonderful and frightening at the same time.

~ ~ ~

Nathalie Müller had not been up to the roof. I found this out when we began talking. She was asking for the bottle opener, which I had been guarding jealously – there was only one. As I glanced up to hand it to her, I realized that I was looking at a very beautiful woman. We had not been introduced. So I withheld the bottle opener until such introductions had been made. I mentioned the beautiful view from the rooftop, she mentioned she had not been up there yet, and I pulled her away to go have a look.

When we stepped up out into the open air, it was nice to get a chance to touch her elbow as I guided her around the random cables on the ground, over to the edge of the roof. I had already forgotten that my friends were leaving soon. The view from the rooftop was magnificent, and we talked easily.

Nathalie was from Switzerland. Working in New Jersey, as part of some business college study-abroad program. She was 23, my age – tall, blonde, beautiful. She told me about her adventures in the city, places she had been where I should go. Places we had both been. How much she loved the Village where I lived. I was new to New York myself, maybe as new as she was.

A friend of hers came over to interrupt us. He was one of the other Swiss exchange students. Obviously jealous. I'm not just saying that, it *was* obvious. Obviously she had no interest in him. These weren't difficult signals to read. Nathalie introduced us politely, and he shook my hand overly hard and looked me challengingly in the eyes. Then she ignored him, and so did I. He didn't have much to add to our conversation.

~   ~   ~

When I got back to my apartment, I fell to the ground and cried. Wailed. Prayed hysterically. I went into shock, shivering and gasping for air. Convulsing on the ground. And in between that, I punched things until my knuckles were bruised and aching. Early the next morning, I called Nathalie and left another message on her voicemail.

"Hi Nathalie, I was calling one more time to wish you a safe trip. I hope you were able to get out and have a nice time last night. I feel bad not to go to the airport to see you off, but I really couldn't watch you fly away. I would do something crazy if I was there, jump past security, try to make you stay. Listen, when you get on that plane today, even at the last minute, if you decide you don't want to leave, don't leave. You can still come back and stay with me. I mean, if you have to leave — but you don't have to leave. Don't leave me. Don't do it. Don't leave me."

My voice broke, and I couldn't say any more.

But she had to leave.

~   ~   ~

"Mothfire By Night"

And there we sat,
Two moths to the same flame,
And only two to our flame.

Somehow our hearts caught fire,

And the fire drew us in,
And our two bodies beckoned the all enflaming wind.

Somehow.

My Love,
So strong you are to leave the flame.
How can you?
I am caught here in the wind,
The wind blows cold without you,
And still I twist and spin.

My Love,
Come back and teach me how to ride the wind with you,
So it summons up the flames again –
Which is naught that need be taught, only to be with you.
Teach me we can ride the wind together,
And forever I will ride the winds with you.

You have flown away and this wind has grown so cold.
And still I twist and spin, caught within the wind within,

My Love. My Love.

~　　~　　~

I remember walking through Soho with Nathalie. We were talking about New York, I guess, the different neighborhoods. I told her how Soho was filled with fashion boutiques and beautiful girls. How I had walked down here on a Saturday during Fashion Week and every girl on the street was the most beautiful girl I had ever seen. Like some alien, fantasy planet. Another world.

Nathalie became tense. Almost defensive. And I could tell she was trying to hide it. She looked away as I was talking. Looked back again. And finally stared at me inquisitively.

"Really? That is very strange."

"They weren't as pretty as you, of course," I continued, and she relaxed immediately.

~   ~   ~

She wanted us to keep in touch. I didn't think we would, but we have. Just the occasional phone call or e-mail, one way or the other. Bittersweet, I would have avoided it. But the desire to hear her voice, to connect again, even barely – overrides anything else.

It's always the same when I talk to her. Always so easy and natural. So charming, good for my spirit. I punch things after I hang up the phone. Sometimes I still cry. And that's not like me. We didn't have much time together, we didn't have that, but there was never a single, isolated moment when I would reach out my hand to her, that she was not also reaching out to me.

~   ~   ~

I sent Nathalie an e-mail the next day. I worked really hard on it. I did my best to be friendly, kind, gracious, yet still present a subtly sexual front in order to avoid the "just friends" zone. I had visited that zone before. Haven't we all?

After not hearing back for a week, I tried to call her. Or,

I had tried originally, but could not get the call to connect. Not that the number was phony, just that in the routing to Switzerland and back, it would always get lost. I think I eventually figured it out and got her voicemail. Anyway, I didn't hear back.

Which was too bad, but not entirely unexpected. With Nathalie things had gone so well and easily, though. Or maybe that's why.

I couldn't stop thinking about her. Told my friends, "The Swiss girl mind fucked me." Which is to say, that I could not get her out of my mind, or stop checking my e-mail obsessively to see if she had replied. Or take any kind of interest in any of the other girls around. Which is to say that my last small shred of romantic confidence had been obliterated. Which is to say that again and again I looked back over the e-mail I had sent to try to figure out what I had done wrong. Which is to say that I didn't want to tell my friends any of this, so I just said, "The Swiss girl mind fucked me."

Luckily, I had a lot going on in my life at the time. I had just moved to a new city, I had just started law school; there were a lot of new faces, new experiences, new fun to be had, new obstacles to overcome. I had hoped, and so there were. After two weeks of chagrin I forgot about "the Swiss girl".

But I left her number on my phone. Coded it to ring in an orange color. That was the VIP color, you see. She was the first VIP in my phonebook. I created the VIP category just for her. Ringing in orange meant the woman of your dreams was on the phone – she must have been very important, since she didn't call.

~   ~   ~

Of course I asked her to marry me. I was frightened to ask. Not frightened to marry her. Of that I had not the slightest doubt. Frightened that she would think me crazy to ask. Frightened that she would take it for a joke and laugh.

She didn't.

Nathalie just stood in silence, staring away, like she didn't know what to do. Like she had been afraid of this, or, not of it, exactly, but of what to do about it. Like she had hoped she didn't have to choose.

"Do you even consider it?" I wondered, seeking some kind of validation.

"Yes, of course. I consider it. I consider it, but is it even possible? What would your family think?"

I had to laugh. What *would* they think?

"My family? They will be worried about it, but then they will say, 'Oh, we always knew that Justin would do something like this.' They will love you because I love you. And when they know you, they'll love you. I do love you, you know."

"Justin…"

"I know we haven't had much time, but… Look, I can tell you everything bad about myself."

"Justin."

"It's nothing terrible."

"I'm sure it's not."

"Yeah, we haven't had that much time, but I think, when you find something so special like this, you have to hold onto it. What we have, the feelings we have together, it's something that most people in the world never get to have! I feel like, the thing with your boyfriend back in Switzerland, if that was what was meant for you, if that was right in your life, then you wouldn't be here with me right now. You were meant to be with me. Don't you feel it? You should stay here with me. It will be hard, I'm not saying it won't be hard, but it will be wonderful.

I took a deep breath and looked into her eyes. She was crying.

"I don't ever want to say goodbye to you," I concluded simply.

We talked about immigration, about how we would get to see her family in Switzerland, and my family back in Oregon. About how we would survive. And I spun beautiful stories of our future together – it wasn't hard to do.

Mostly we just cried in each other's arms. A couple of hours later, Nathalie said she couldn't do it, and that she had to go.

~ ~ ~

Early in the morning I called and got her voicemail. Time was running out on me, on us, and I felt it. I didn't know what to do.

"Nathalie, this is Justin. Listen, I don't know what the future is, for me, or for you, or for anyone. And I don't know what all your situation is, and I wish I did, but I don't. All I know, is that right now you're in New York, and I'm in New York, and I feel like we should be together. Don't you feel that? When I'm with you it's like magic — like everything is right in the world. And when I look into your eyes I think you feel it too. I can't tell you what to do, or what you should do, or what is best for you. I can only tell you how I feel, and what I think, and when I look inside and listen to my heart everything

screams out that we should spend this time together. I mean, when you look inside, what does your heart tell you?"

She called me back an hour later.

"Hello, Justin? Yes, hi, it's Nathalie. I'm sorry I did not call you sooner, I was in late last night and I only just got up. But I got your voicebox message, it was very fine. I think we will meet today, yes?"

~   ~   ~

We walked back to my apartment to send the night off with "some coffee or something". The rain had disappeared; on this clear, beautiful night we had the streets to ourselves. I kept my arms around Nathalie as we laughed and embraced and whispered our way through the city.

I think those were the happiest moments of my life.

Nathalie was so funny and sweet, and smart in a quirky kind of way. She loved colloquial English expressions, and was keen to memorize them all. We talked about languages. New York, Switzerland, Niagara Falls – but each other mostly. Who we were and where we came from, and why.

And I'd never even kissed a girl before so I was trying to work that out in my head. What to do when we got back to my apartment. How I could avoid making a fool out of myself. Of course, I wanted to make love to this beautiful, sweet, feminine creature. But I didn't want it to be something she would regret. Nor did I want Nathalie to realize how innocent I was.

I was innocent, but not naïve, and Nathalie accepted me as I presented myself. She never tried to keep me from being the person that I wanted to be. For me that was unique.

We got back to my apartment, and I put some violin music on in the background. I hated for Nathalie to see my apartment. It didn't seem good enough for her. Not compared to the rest of the neighborhood. I'd told her that I lived in Greenwich Village, off of 5th Avenue, but I didn't tell her it was student housing.

Nathalie would have none of it. She said she loved the place, and it felt like she was saying that she just loved being there with me.

~   ~   ~

We arranged to meet in Union Square. It was a miserable night – raining very hard, and windy. I worried about how Nathalie was getting on. I made my way to the designated bookstore a few minutes early, and presented myself with a problem: I could not remember what Nathalie looked like. Not exactly, at least. The more I tried to picture her face, the more fuzzy it became. Suddenly all I could remember was that she was tall, blonde, and rather pretty. It didn't seem like enough. Could she be here and me not recognize her? I glanced furtively at the women around me.

Eventually my cell phone rang. "Hello, Justin? Yes, I am here, where are you?" And she was there, standing behind me, in the entranceway outside the store. Beautiful as ever, and unmistakable. I walked back through the doors and hugged her, and we kissed on both cheeks in the European style. I was beginning to like that style.

~   ~   ~

I can't let her walk away from me.

The thought echoed in my mind again and again. Mad ideas began swimming in my brain. I started asking Nathalie disqualificatory questions. Things to test her, that might help me to let go. To say, "Well, there was this thing about her that I really couldn't have lived with, anyway." But every answer was warm, and sweet, and thoughtful – and drew me in deeper.

What could I do? Considering Nathalie's situation back home and what an attractive girl she was, a long distance relationship seemed impossible. We hadn't had enough time. No, if she walked away from me now, I would never see her again. The thought killed me.

She couldn't stay and live in New York with me, because her visa was expiring. Beyond everything else, I mean. Even if she would. Anyway, I didn't want that kind of relationship. I'm a moral, religious person. The thought that she was running around with me behind her boyfriend's back was already almost more than I could accept. With any other girl I would never have gotten into such a situation. I needed to believe that the same was true for her. That with any other man she would not be in this predicament. Because – or else, how could I ever trust her?

And so what if she moved in with me and we slept together and were happy until – until when? When things ended and she moved on? Until nothing. Until slain by a guilty, insecure love. That can neither be resisted, nor trusted. Love will deal a killing blow.

I didn't want to ever say goodbye to Nathalie. I didn't want to ever get up in the morning and not see her. To have good or bad in her life and me not be there. Her not to be there in my own. Or have any kind of sweetness and not share it. To brush across true love and fail to bear it.

~   ~   ~

I could never go to Switzerland to visit Nathalie, though I would. She is with her boyfriend there. Can you imagine? She told me to come, but I'm not sure what she was thinking. She wasn't going to leave her boyfriend. She said she wanted it to be, "like it was when I was in New York." I don't even know what that means.

Nathalie has wanted to come see me in New York, as well. But never made it back. I would have her here, of course. In a second. The boyfriend thing would be hard to swallow, though. I would pretend he didn't exist. Would she? It's not in my nature to play games behind someone's back. I don't understand it.

Reality creeps in. I remember that she spent her last evening in New York with an Italian man, not with me. I remember that she has a boyfriend back home. That she always had a boyfriend. For eight years now. And she still wants me to call her. But she's never called me.

My love. My Nathalie. I could never resist her. Or think a bad thought about her. To me she is perfect. Even if she is flawed.

~   ~   ~

We sat together and talked and whispered. Things continued as they had been before. Nathalie still refused to kiss me, but everything else escalated at an alarming rate. It all seemed so inevitable – yet, fragile. A delicate, powerful spell. Chemistry so palpable. My senses were on edge; intoxicated.

Do you know how women smell? Fresh and clean. No chemicals or scents. Just natural human flesh. Like the world has just begun and there's no dirtiness yet. It smells like life. Life living more than birth. Like the Garden of Eden. It smells like Eve. Like perfection. And you can touch it.

In my life, that was Nathalie. The perfection that I could touch. I felt so blessed. Wanted to ravish her, of course. But I would never cast dirt on that face. Or greet that being regretful in the morning. So we moved fast, but slow. And I just held her, and touched her, and kissed her skin. Pulled the shift off of her shoulders. And watched her eyes. Blue pools overcome with black. And she assented or resisted as she would. That was fine.

As we skirted some edge of no return, the music abruptly stopped. The machine gave up spontaneously. I couldn't get it playing again, and we were overcome by sudden, overwhelming silence. Like we had been cast into space and the only reference point was our voices and it was all a bit disturbing. Like the hand of God had come down, cut the music, and said, "Enough." Nathalie twitched, like a switch had flipped inside her brain.

"I think I go now," she said firmly and immediately prepared to leave.

"You don't have to leave," I protested. My protective instincts started kicking in and I did not want her going home alone so late at night. It was two or three in the morning. And I sure as hell didn't want her to leave anyway. "You can stay here tonight, I'll sleep on the floor."

"No, no, I go now," she said again, pulling on her second boot. Not even like she was telling me, like she was telling herself.

Nathalie apologized as she walked out the door. She hoped I wasn't mad at her. I know what she meant, and it hurt, but, Lord, how could I be mad at that girl?

~   ~   ~

What did you think I could have done? What did you think I could do? Weren't my hands tied?

"So now you'll go back to Switzerland, and you won't even kiss me goodbye?"

"Justin –"

"So you can tell your boyfriend you didn't even kiss anyone?" I asked bitterly, trying to sound merely skeptical.

"Yes, Justin, you know, I am sorry, it is hard but this is the situation I am in."

"I should be your boyfriend."

"Justin, you don't understand. If he was my boyfriend for a month, or for six months, then I would say, yes, I have met you now and that is over and I am with you. But Maximillian and I, we have been together for six years!"

~   ~   ~

Nathalie ordered breakfast while I sipped some tea; I had already eaten.

As we sat there talking, Nathalie rested her feet on top of mine. It was the most charming thing. Like an accident, except it wasn't. No nudging, or rubbing, or tapping, just her feet set there, matter of factly, on top of mine. As if to say, "That's where they go." She would smile and twinkle her eyes at me; I must have done the same. I would never kick those feet off. Not in a million years. Or even nudge one from its place.

Nathalie worked some as a waitress back home, so we talked about salaries, and taxes, and tipping – mundane things, but it all seemed so interesting if I was talking to her about it. The food was good, I was glad, and the time flashed past us. She had to leave soon. As we walked back to my apartment, I put my arm around her and she didn't pull away.

~   ~   ~

"Listen to me," I said into her ear as I held her, "You're a very special person. You deserve someone wonderful in your life. Even if it's not me. I'm not saying me. Whatever you do, find someone who really makes you happy. Be good to yourself. Because life's too short."

Nathalie squeezed my hands tightly, close to tears.

"You are too, Justin. You too, ok?"

I watched her walk into her hotel, open the doors, walk up the stairs, and that was the last time I saw her. Something salty stained my face as I shuffled back down the street. Spurning the subway, I moved into the darkness of Central Park. It was finally night, black. I didn't look behind me. What did I have to lose? I hoped I would get mugged. Have someone to fight.

~   ~   ~

Then one night she called me. Late at night, on a Sunday. I think I jumped when I looked down and saw my phone lit up in orange. Did I still have that number on there? My hand trembled as I picked up the phone.

"Hello?"

It had only been 16 days since I met her. I know this, because I have digitally dated photographs from both days. But I wouldn't have believed that if you told me. I had to go back and check to find out. In the back of my mind I still wonder if those dates are wrong. Those two weeks must have been two months. At the time, they seemed like ages.

"Hello, yes, Justin? This is Nathalie Müller. Hi! Yes, I'm so sorry I did not get back to you sooner, but I have been visiting Canada with my company, yes, and have been very busy with work and getting ready to move back to Switzerland. But I got your e-mails, they were fine – nothing wrong, so to say, and now, tomorrow, I am coming back into New York. Yes, so maybe we could meet in Greenwich Village like you say."

Her English was actually pretty good for someone who had only been here a few months. She was so sweet. It's hard to convey in text. There was a natural, tender cheer in her voice. So easy with me. It was like every word of every sentence was right with her. My irritation evaporated painlessly into the air.

~　　~　　~

As we walked to the subway, things were awkward between us for the first time. Neither of us knew what to say, so we just made small talk. Nathalie had missed her meeting with her cousin and the Italian fellow, so she was arranging to see them later that night. I found it difficult to accept, and tried to get her to spend that last time with me, but I think we both knew that couldn't happen. She needed to go home, shower, change. Saying goodbye was too hard in the first place.

We tried our best to make small talk, but didn't know what to talk about. Stupid things like what books and movies we liked. The people on the subway seemed out of place, like they shouldn't be there. I wanted to wrap my arms around Nathalie, to kiss her, touch her, anything. But couldn't.

Then we got to talking again, and everything was back the way it was. For a moment.

On the street outside her hotel, I kissed Nathalie on both cheeks and hugged her tightly for the last time.

~ ~ ~

She came downtown to meet me the next morning. The buzzer on my building was broken, so I went downstairs to let her in. Standing on the other side of the glass, beautiful as ever; I couldn't open the door quickly enough. We hugged each other tight.

Nathalie was trying to see everyone and do everything in New York that she had not gotten a chance to see and do while working. She was sort of squeezing me into her schedule, and I, for my part, was dispensing with anything in my week that could conflict with a chance to see her. Missing things that I could scarcely afford to miss.

There was a cute little café close by, so we headed there to get some food. As we walked down the street, everyone stared at Nathalie. Greenwich Village is a neighborhood full of beautiful women, and, still, everyone stared and smiled and grinned at her. And she stood close to me. And I felt a bit smug.

But mostly I felt blessed. Here was the most wonderful girl I had ever met, and she wanted to spend her time with me. Why?

~   ~   ~

We could only hang out for a few minutes before she had to leave. Nathalie was meeting her cousin and then later an Italian fellow she had made friends with when she first arrived. This caused me considerable discontent. I couldn't figure what to say. She told me about the guy, made it sound innocent, but I was unconvinced.

"That Italian guy just wants to get in your pants," I finally proffered, awkwardly, and Nathalie laughed.

"What? In my pants? What does it mean?"

Shit. It was hard for me to say that in the first place, and now I had to explain it. I had to laugh, though.

"Get in your pants. It means, like, he just wants to have sex with you."

Nathalie giggled uncontrollably, "Oh, it's so funny."

She loved the phrase, and told me there was a similar expression in German. All the quirky American phrases, slang, and expressions delighted her and she was eager to learn them. It was something very charming about her. The way these little things delighted. Most people are too hard to be delighted by little things in life, even when these are the things that are the most delightful. I remember Nathalie being so happy about a wonderful new expression she had learned, "chilling in my crib". I didn't have the heart to tell her it had gone out of style long before.

"Oh, you're jealous?" she asked, hugging me affectionately.

"Of course I'm jealous! I don't want you spending your
time in New York with some other guy. I want you to be
spending all your time with me."

"Awww, you're so cute."

I didn't know how to respond to that. 'Cute' – it got
under my skin.

"Thanks," I said, attempting to sound disingenuous.

"Well if he tries to 'get in my pants'," Nathalie continued, suppressing another giggle, "I will say, 'no, my friend
Justin would be very upset.' "

~   ~   ~

Nathalie was insistent that we meet the next day. Not
that she was pressuring me or anything, it just seemed to be
important to her that we should meet as soon as possible.
She was moving back to Switzerland on Thursday. She
called me on Sunday. We would meet on Monday. Right?
She was very concerned about it. I was a little bit flattered.

So we made plans to meet the next day, but she was
delayed on her train into the city. She called me, upset and
very apologetic. "We will still meet tonight, though, yes?"
That was her, not me. Of course we would.

~   ~   ~

She collected her things together and we sat again for a
moment on my bed.

"I don't want you to go, I want you to stay here with me
forever."

"Awww, you're so cute," Nathalie said for the dozenth time, and squeezed me to her.

One too many times, I couldn't take it anymore.

"You know, it's fine for you to say that," I responded with forced detachment, "but it doesn't make me feel very good."

"What?" Nathalie stared at me, confused.

"To always say I am 'cute', you know, it makes me feel emasculated, like you are talking to a little boy."

Nathalie looked genuinely mortified. Really upset. She drew back from me, the color drained from her face, and she struggled to find words.

"Justin, that is not what I mean. When I say this to you – you know, these things are, are very special to me. It means something special to me to be with you, and when you say these things or do these things, my heart goes, 'oh', you see? How would you say this in English, when something is very special to you and you are affected by it?"

How would you say it in English? I'm a writer and I'm not sure that I know. You could say you are moved, or touched, that your heart is warmed – you could get close. Perhaps the best you could do is, "I love you." But sometimes you can't say it, and sometimes it's not the same thing. I just hugged her and apologized, and tried to think of ways to express what she had said. We talked about it, and laughed a little bit. For a few moments we forgot we were saying goodbye.

~   ~   ~

At some point when I knew her, I was walking with Nathalie and I said something about when she has children.

131

She responded by saying, "Oh, Justin, I don't know, but maybe I have missed that, that train in my life." And it really upset me. Not for myself, but for Nathalie. Because she was such an affectionate person. Gently wise. The kind of woman who should be a mother, who will find the best kind of peace and joy in that. And for the world's sake. I mean, it seems like the wonderful people in this life owe a duty to the rest of us to propagate themselves. Beautiful, sweet, kind-hearted people are dreadfully rare in each instance, let alone in combination.

For a girl like that not to have children. Not to be a Momma. Not to have that, and give that to the world. What a tragedy. It still upsets me.

~   ~   ~

"ALSO YOUR OWN"

My Love,
You are so strong to resist the flame.
How can you?

My Love,
You surely feel what I feel.
How can you?

My Love,
It can't be easy for you.
How can you?

My Love,
It feels so cold without you.
How can you?

My Love,
Help me find my way to you.
How can you?

My Love,
Forgive me for my love.
How can you?

My Love,
Love me too.
How can you be so strong when you love me too?

~   ~   ~

Nathalie was thinking of visiting me again this past March. That's the last time I spoke with her. We hadn't talked in months, which was normal. I caught her on the phone just as she was walking out the door. Moving. Everything was packed away in her car. She had a new job, in a new city. Berne, where her boyfriend lived. She was finally moving in with him. She was sorry, but she had to go.

Two years ago I met a girl named Nathalie Müller. She e-mailed me again the other night. I'm writing this now, because I don't know what to say.

CHAPTER 8

ADAM ROSE EARLY to start work the next morning. Eve sat alone in the field, already waiting for him. An early rising butterfly fluttered its wings on her finger, bright colors subdued in the grey morning light. Eve laughed, marveled, and blew on it in turns.

"Eve!" Adam exclaimed, catching sight of her.

The butterfly alighted at the disturbance. Eve snapped her fingers together cheerfully and looked up smiling.

"Hello," she said.

"Good morning," Adam said, "You're up very early."

"Oh? I always get up early."

Adam bent and squeezed her shoulder, and kissed her on the head.

"It's not so very early is it? The sun is already coming into the sky," Eve commented.

"No, you're right, but still. You're back already! I feared I would have to wait weeks to see you again."

Eve laughed.

"I hope not, Adam," she said sincerely, "I would hate that."

They were both grinning.

"So, when do we start planting?" Eve finally wondered.

"Oh? You're going to help me?"

"That was the plan."

"It seems an excellent plan to me," Adam said. "I haven't yet finished sowing all the seed for the furrows, do you think you could help with that?"

"Of course."

Two narrow streaks of sunlight broke across Eve's pretty face, dividing it into bands of color and grey. She sat thinking, looking at the ground. So beautiful. Adam could not stop staring at her. Marveling that such a creature should be happy to see him.

"Then let's get started straight away," he said finally, thinking of nothing else to say.

"Yes, let's."

Eve stood up. She yawned and stretched, then smiled at the breaking sun and leaned against Adam, resting her head against his chest. He put his arms around her and buried his nose in her hair, breathing deeply. She could hear the heart within his breast.

"Oh, I've forgotten something," Adam said abruptly, "I have something for you."

"For me?" Eve scrutinized his face, as if it would betray the surprise.

"Can you wait here a moment, I'll just run and get it."

"I'm not going anywhere, Adam."

"Right, well, right, just don't."

They both found humor in this and Adam sprinted excitedly back to the tower. He returned a few minutes later, clutching something in one fist, concealing what it was.

"It's not much, but, here," he says, holding out the onyx and jade necklace.

"Adam, I don't know what — for me?"

Eve lifts the necklace out of his hands and cradles it preciously in her own. Perhaps she expected another apple.

"It's beautiful. You made this?"

"I did," Adam nods, "Do you like it?"

Sunlight peeks from the far horizon, catching and illuminating the necklace. The jade glows, the onyx takes on infinite depth. The carving of each bead stands in relief distinctly. A breeze catches and twists the necklace in Eve's hand, and a shining coat of sheen dances up and down along it.

"Of course I like it. I think— It's the most beautiful necklace I have ever seen. Too much of a gift for me to accept."

"Here," Adam says, taking the necklace out of Eve's hands and clasping it quickly around her neck. "Necklaces are meant to be worn, after all."

Eve rubs the stones, half unconsciously, half warily, against her neck. Half caressingly.

"Thank you, Adam. I don't know what to say."

"Say nothing. I'm just happy you like it."

Soon enough, they began their work. As they worked, they talked, of course, and as they talked they each began to learn who this person was, whom they already loved.

Eve was the next to youngest daughter of a large family. Her father was a philosopher; important, so she said, but poor. From a young age she had taken to wandering in the forest alone. It was a peculiar habit, even for an Atlantean, but one her parents had found impossible to dissuade her of. The great forest was separated from Atlantis by a deep chasm in the earth, difficult to cross. It was enshrouded in mists of superstition, profound barriers compared to natural water and air. Few Atlanteans ventured into it.

By her own account, Eve knew the forest better than anyone else. As a teenager she would wander there from home, and began to spend days at a time by herself in the wild. Her parents' horror was diminished somewhat when Eve started to bring back precious herbs and delicacies that could be sold in the city market. This became a genuine livelihood, and allowed her to live with a freedom that matched her very independent nature.

Eve's lifestyle had its drawbacks, however. She was viewed as an outsider by many of those in her community. Some viewed her as a pariah. After spending so much time alone, and in such a different context from other girls in the city, Eve found it difficult to relate to many of her peers, or even to communicate with them at all. Their social networks were governed by a code she did not understand. Universally acknowledged as special, Eve had few friends. And, as well, she was very proud.

Which made her life difficult now that she was coming into the marrying age. Eve confessed to Adam that she had little hope of making a good match. She mentioned it matter of factly, sitting watching him work in his field at the end of a long day. Her parents, she said, had told her not to get her hopes too high. With her wild nature, and peculiar habits, there were few young men in Atlantis who would want her for a wife.

Adam snorted indignantly at this. He said it was ridiculous, of course.

"The few that would have me," Eve said, "would probably marry me for the wrong reasons. As a kind of slave, gathering bounty in the forest to support them. Or else because, well, I'm not *bad* looking, after all. Maybe some would consider me their best chance of marrying a pretty girl, and be willing to overlook the rest. Probably believing they can 'cure' me."

"Do the men themselves have that much choice?" Adam wondered. "Surely their families are the ones who really matter."

"Well, I'm not sure about that. I don't entirely understand the process, but if it is the families who will be choosing me then that is even worse! Then they would surely only choose me for a slave! Life would be better without a match at all."

"Don't say that," Adam admonished her, "you don't want to live out your life alone."

"How would you know what I want?"

"At least, it doesn't seem like it," he continued patiently. "You could be matched with someone like me, would that be so terrible?"

"There's nobody like you in Atlantis," Eve said flatly.

"No, perhaps not. Well... Well, I won't try to convince you otherwise. It doesn't give me any pleasure to imagine you matched back home with some other man."

"Oh, ho. So possessive already," Eve smiled at him.

Adam met her smile sternly, surprised at the anger welling up inside of him. He looked away, then, looking up, he saw the smile again, and it cut into him, surgically, excising things inside him. And the anger was gone. Then he smiled back. Then he looked down and was mad again. Eve stopped smiling and bit her lip, staring at him curiously. As Adam pulled a deeply rooted weed out of the ground, his hand trembled. He threw it down in disgust, then turned back to Eve, summoning all of his inner courage.

"I'm not far from being matched myself," he said. "And if you want to know the truth, I'm considered the best of the young men in York. I will match very, very well. And, if you want to know the truth, I could only dream of being matched with a girl like you. I *do* dream of being matched with a girl like you. And you are the only girl like you that I have ever met, and probably that there ever is. Or even is. And– You shouldn't sell yourself so cheaply, even in talk."

Eve caught her breath and blushed. They worked in silence for a while.

Gazpacho [that's soup]

"I don't really know why this story is so long, because
there's not that much in it."

Not exactly a concerto, more of a parlor piece that got out of
hand. I mean what happened to the protagonist and this
relationship, not the writing itself. The writing itself doesn't
even merit publishing, how did it end up in your hands? From
out of mine? Apologies in advance.

It's kind of boring and the same thing over and over again.

This story is a comedy. Supposed to be.

2/6

I MET DELIA IN a bar, at the birthday party of a friend of a friend of a friend. That would make Delia a friend of a friend of a friend of a friend. Which is a tenuous relationship, at best. It was kind of weird, too, because there were only about eight people at that party. But there were a lot of people in the bar.

Weird, I mean, because we saw each other on the other side of the bar before we met. Made eye contact or something. She was a cute girl, and I thought I would keep my eye out for her as the night went on. After struggling through the crowd, I squeezed in with the rest of our group and was surprised to find her seated right beside me. She acted a little interested, and I told her that I wasn't with her friends at all, but rather trying to bluff my way into the group.

Delia got sort of confused and flustered by this, but she seemed willing to accept whatever I said. Which was cool, and I'm glad I'm a nice person. We introduced ourselves and pretty soon I told her I was kidding around, and really was part of the group, so we chatted and flirted, and it was easy.

Eventually everyone wanted to leave the place, which was fine, although I can't say what the problem with it was. Just crowded and loud, but there was a good mix of people, so to me it was good.

I think some of my friends wanted me to hook up with the birthday girl. At least that's what they said. She and I were a good match or something. Anyway, I found Delia to be much more attractive at the time, so I mostly just ignored the birthday girl and talked to her. She was very intelligent and sophisticated, an intriguing conversationalist. And she had this bottled up, feminine build that was dead sexy. Cute face, too. And I caught sight of her tight, smooth, silky tummy, curving down inside her pants as she stood next to me for a minute. Grrrrr!

When we got outside, a good friend had some weird psychotic meltdown and started aggressively informing me that he could kick my ass. I didn't know what to do except laugh, but that didn't help. He would call up the next morning to scream at me and threaten some more. Inform me that those were all his friends, not mine. Somehow we managed to stay buddies after that, but I could never really trust him again. So it would be fair to say that Delia actually cost me one of my closest friends. Ok, maybe not fair, but I'll say it anyway. For effect.

Delia and the birthday girl started heading to another club, fast, so I just stuck with them and enjoyed myself, pushing the thought of any potential "ass beatings" out of my mind. All angry people were left behind. Not that I was worried, just, well, I hadn't really had anyone get threatening towards me like that since high school. I don't usually inspire animosity in others. These new friends of mine were agreeable, and pretty, and it's fun to walk down the street with agreeable, pretty women. Especially in New York. Delia's friend, the birthday girl, was a Tall Scandinavian Blonde, so that was bonus.

Now that I think about it, I usually go for Tall Scandinavian Blondes. I guess Delia was something special.

Delia and I sat at the club with everyone else, but only talked to each other. That was nice, especially since I was the outsider in the group that was left. I think she got up to go smoke once or twice and other than that we talked the whole time. Anyway, she was trying to cover up her smoker breath by chewing Big Red gum. Our faces were very close together as we talked, almost intimate.

"I walked by these flowers in Central Park today, and they smelled so beautiful," Delia commented to me. "Not really like anything I've ever smelled before. Just, voluptuously luscious."

"You know what I smell," I asked devilishly, looking intently into her eyes.

"What?"

"Big Red."

I winked at her, and her face flushed a little bit, and I think she almost swallowed the gum. I wasn't trying to be insulting, though. I happen to like the smell of big red, and she offered me a piece, but I declined. My drink didn't go well with chewing gum, whatever it was.

Delia talked on at great length about the Kennedys and some other famous rich family she was reading about. Or maybe researching, I'm not sure. That should have been a warning sign. Should have ejected then. Maybe. I mean, it was great to have a conversation with an intelligent, educated, thoughtful person, but I sort of tend to think that the entire Kennedy clan should be dragged out into the street and executed. God seems to think so too.

No; bad joke, sorry about that.

Delia was charming. We made arrangements to meet the next weekend. Saturday.

2/14

...I had had no idea that Saturday was Valentine's Day!

When I eventually realized this I sort of freaked out. It seemed so clichéd , and I had never been on a date on Valentine's day before. I wondered if Delia had realized what day we were going out on, but, then, she was a girl after all. She must have known. I wondered what she would expect, and realized I would have to buy her flowers or something, and then I thought maybe I should just reschedule the date for another day, but then I thought that was really lame, and realized that I was actually excited to be going out on Valentine's day, and even more so to see Delia again.

I figured I would just let things be cool, buy a rose and give it to her, nothing too dramatic. I passed a rose seller late in the morning.

"Beautiful roses, man, come on. Buy one."

"Um…"

"$5, long stem, beautiful roses, just look at them, you won't get a better deal than this."

"Umm… like, if I buy a rose now, uh, it will still be good tonight, right?"

"Of course!"

"I mean, it won't wilt or anything will it?"

"Come on, man, be serious. I'll wrap it up for you."

"Ok, sure, thanks."

So I had my rose to give to Delia, and spent the rest of the day just sitting around worrying about the night. Trying to figure out what I would wear. Hmm… Something nice.

Delia came and met me at my apartment that night, I don't remember why. She had insisted. I buzzed her up, and grabbed the rose, to hand it to her when I answered the door. What about a greeting, should I hand the rose to her and then kiss her on the cheek, or kiss her on the cheek and then hand her the rose, or? Should I go for the peck on the lips?

When I finally opened the door I think I handed the rose to her and then kissed her cheek. Delia was gracious about it, I'm sure I needn't have worried.

I was a bit taken aback by her appearance, though. Maybe she hadn't realized, when we made arrangements, that this was going to be on Valentine's day? Delia still looked pretty, but she was dressed very… casually. No make-up. Baggy pants and a big, old sweatshirt or something like that – covered up with frump from head to toe. For a second I had to look closely at her face to make sure this was the same girl.

She had made no effort at all. In fact, she seemed to have made a conscious attempt to appear as casual and unattractive as possible. I noticed this resigned look on her face, like, "Let's get it over with. I can't believe I'm here."

Shit, I started to feel the same way.

I tried my best to conceal my discouragement, and we headed uptown to see the movie. We had a nice time chatting on our way up town, but Delia kept a lot of distance between us physically, and her body language towards me was entirely negative. On the subway she leaned up against some random dirty guy [I don't mean figuratively, I mean literally: he was dirty.] in order to squeeze farther away from me. And I wasn't exactly crowding her space. It was disconcerting, and sort of insulting too.

When we finally got into the movie, Delia squeezed up on the far side of her seat, as far away from me as possible, for the whole two and a half hours. I just thought, "Ok, well, that's that. As soon as this movie's over, I'm the fuck out of here." I thought about getting up and leaving right there during the movie. Luckily, or unluckily, it was a good show.

Another thing was, that kind of sucked, as soon as we stepped outside my apartment and started moving around, the rose I had given Delia started drooping over and falling apart. It looked really pathetic, and I told Delia she could just throw it away or whatever, but she insisted on hanging onto it. The first good sign of the evening. But every time I looked over, I would see this pretty girl holding this droopy, pathetic rose, watch another dying petal float to the ground, and for some reason feel like a jackass.

Delia still seemed very distant from me as we got up to leave the theater. It was becoming irritating. As we walked outside, she kept going on and on about how beautiful the actress in the film was. I couldn't figure out what she was getting at. Did she want my opinion?

"She's certainly a pretty girl."

"I just thought she was incredibly beautiful and sexy," Delia repeated.

"Well, you live in New York, maybe you will get a chance to ask her out sometime."

I think that pissed her off. Delia's face burned a bit red, and she turned to me like she was shocked or something.

"I think a woman can think another woman is attractive without there being anything dirty or sexual about it," she said carefully.

"I think so too. I was just kidding you."

"Oh."

Somehow that broke the ice, and we carried on more warmly again afterwards, like when we had first met.

Somehow, as well, it was 11:30 p.m. and neither of us had eaten since lunch. Due to multiple severe food allergies I usually can't eat in social situations, so going without food for long periods of time isn't that weird for me. But usually I'm the only one. I could hear Delia's stomach growl.

"Let's go get some food," she said, and it seemed like a good idea.

We headed over to a nearby kosher Chinese food joint where I thought I could probably find something to eat without accidentally killing myself. Kosher restaurants control the mixing of their ingredients carefully. Unfortunately, the place was only sort of nearby, about 10 blocks away. Even more unfortunately, it was closed when we got there. Delia was really hurting for some food, and even I was starting to feel weak and uncomfortable. We assessed our options.

"Where can you eat?" Delia asked.

"Well I can really only eat Chinese and Korean food. Sometimes. And kosher, because they separate the milk. And I can eat vegan. Do you know any other kosher restaurants around here?"

"…No. I would just say we could go back to my place to make something, but I don't think I have any food you can eat."

"Well, if you want to come back downtown, you're welcome to eat at my place, too," I suggested hopefully.

"No. No. Where do you eat when you go out?"

"See, I don't really eat out that much. Sometimes Chinese or Korean... there is a place called Spice downtow-"

"Spice?"

"Yeah, Spice, have you been there? It's really good."

"Of course I know Spice, everyone knows Spice, let's go there," she said determinedly.

"Oh, cool. Yeah, but it's all the way down in Soho, are you sure you can make it?"

"There's another one up here. It's not too far away. Come on, let's go."

Delia began walking rapidly in the other direction and I

hurried after her.

"Oh, awesome. Wow, I never would have thought they have another branch."

"Really?" Delia sounded surprised.

Spice turned out to be about 10 more blocks away. It was really cold outside and we were both so hungry. Even outside on the street Delia's stomach growled audibly. Luckily we were both really enjoying our conversation as we walked. We seemed to get there quickly, although that might have been because Delia was walking really fast.

"Oh no, I think it's closed," Delia said, a note of forced stoicism in her voice.

"Is it?" I asked, still not quite sure where 'it' was.

She ran to the door, almost frantically.

"…They closed at 11:30."

"This is Spice?"

"Yeah..."

She looked at me skeptically.

"Oh, yeah, right."

"What?"

"Um."

"What is it?"

"Uh, yeah, well it's ok, because, um, I was actually talking about a different restaurant."

"What?"

"Yeah… I think the restaurant I was thinking of was actually called 'Rice'."

"What?"

"Damn, I'm really sorry, Delia."

"Rice."

"I feel like an idiot."

"Rice, down in Soho?"

"Yeah… sorry. Listen, maybe just you should go eat

somewhere, this is really ridiculous to put you through this. I could even just sit and watch you eat if you want, it doesn't bother me, I'm used to it."

"Yeah, no, I know Rice. There's definitely only one Rice."

"I was really surprised, it didn't seem like the kind of place that would have another branch."

"Yeah." Delia paused silently, as if summoning some inner reservoir of strength. "No, we'll figure something out. Do you play pool?"

We walked to a nearby pool hall; upscale, Manhattan style. Delia was friends with the night manager, a young man named Aiden, who grinned at her and called her "Peaches". She said she used to play in the leagues here and after a while Aiden had told her to just come whenever she wanted, no charge. She didn't seem to think that was strange or unusual. To me, free pool sounded like a lot of fun.

The pool hall was a big, open, sunken room with dozens of tables and a fully stocked bar area. Everything about it was bright and pleasant. The tables all seemed to have new felt. I don't recall what the rates were, but a lot more than you pay in Oregon. Aiden pointed us to an empty table and said to play as long as we wanted.

Every once in a while in New York you meet these pretty, young women who seem to get everything for free, or if not free then for a special, super, secret rate. Apartments, drinks at a favorite bar — random things, little and big. It's a kind of mystery, because other women, equally beautiful or more, won't get any of that special treatment. Delia was a very cute girl, perhaps "very, very" cute, but you wouldn't say she was particularly beautiful. And I'm pretty sure she wasn't handing out any sexual favors in return. Could be wrong. You never know about that. But you find these certain, special, freebie girls in New York. Maybe everywhere. Maybe it is just good for some businesses to have pretty girls hanging around, like a loss leader.

We started playing pool and neither of us were very good. Maybe Delia was going easy on me. Or maybe she was just so hungry it was interfering with her game. It took us forever to get through the first rack. Long before then, Delia went and got us some free drinks.

All this free stuff made me uneasy, and I kept asking Delia about it.

"I mean, but doesn't it seem kind of weird that they just give you all this stuff for free?"

"No," she said matter of factly, "they like me here."

"But, I mean, usually when people give something for free they really expect something in return."

"Well they can expect whatever they want, but I'm not giving them anything."

"But are you sure," I pressed, "they won't care that I'm getting free stuff, too?"

"Well they gave me the drinks. Aiden doesn't seem to mind."

"Yeah..."

"If you're so worried about it you can go over to the bar and pay for the drinks," Delia said in exasperation

Hmmmmm.

"Well, if you think it's okay, then I'm sure it is," I said, and took a sip from my – whatever it was called.

[I had told Delia to just get me whatever she was drinking, and this turned out to be pretty similar to a gin and tonic. A year later I ordered the same drink from a different bar and was laughed at by the female bartender, who brought back a fruity, syrupy drink with cherries in it and refused to flirt with me anymore for the rest of the night. After that I forgot the name. Permanently.]

Delia and I sat at a little coffee table near our pool table, engrossed in conversation and occasionally sipping at our drinks. Some friends of hers were playing at a table nearby and said 'hi' and ignored us. I don't remember what we talked about. Could make something up, but it doesn't really matter.

"I'll be back in a minute," Delia said abruptly, standing and grabbing her jacket.

"Is everything ok?"

"I'm just, I just have to go outside and have a smoke. Wait here and watch our drinks, please. I'll be right back."

I watched a celebrity midget shooting pool at the next table, but that got boring.

Delia's friends were slightly more interesting. A grey haired, sloppy looking guy, and a younger, pretty, Asian girl. Every few minutes they would stop shooting, stand together by the table, and make out a little bit. It got me to thinking about what I was doing here with Delia. Should I be putting "the moves" on her? She seemed so skittish, I was afraid to push her boundaries. But, she must have been attracted to me to go through all this, to be half starving and still want us to spend more time together. It kept feeling like I knew what I needed to do, but my hands were tied to prevent me doing it. Although... I feel that way a lot.

The courtship ritual of Delia's two friends was awkward. Not that I was staring or anything. There was something profoundly mechanical about it, like a pair of robots acting out programmed sets of motions. The two of them would stand holding each other intimately, yet bereft of visible passions or emotion. Like poor actors. It made you squirm a little bit inside to see it. Or maybe just me.

Delia came back after ten minutes, devouring a basket of pretzels.

We shot some more pool, poorly, but mostly just sat and talked. At least in terms of our conversation the two of us really connected. Every once in a while one of our growling stomachs would interrupt, and we would laugh about it. Then we would try to think of a solution to our food dilemma, but quickly become re-engrossed in whatever we were talking about before.

I would say we could go to a restaurant where at least she could eat. Delia would refuse. She would repeat emphatically how sorry she was that we could not just go to her place to eat something, because the only food she had at home was cheese and ice cream. Then I would offer that we could both go back downtown and eat at my place, but she would say that was "not a good idea." It was getting very late, no grocery stores were still open, and few restaurants. I would tell her that I was having a good time, but would understand if she wanted to call it a night. She would insist against it.

We sat talking like that in the pool hall for two or three hours. Some movie star, Matt somebody or other, came and went and everyone tittered, pretending not to stare.

I couldn't concentrate enough for meaningful conversation after a while. Too hungry. Delia's pretty little face looked grey. She regretfully concluded that she needed to go home and eat the cheese and ice cream she had there. Also, I think, a lasagna tv dinner or something. I was at the breaking point as well, and couldn't wait to get home and fix some food.

It was hard to know what to make of our date. Presumably for both of us. One could almost call it a disaster, but

I'd actually had a pretty good time. Delia didn't seem to be unhappy with me at all, or even irritated. Just very, very hungry. I really respected her for that. Not being unhappy with me, I mean.

Delia lived eight or ten blocks from the pool hall, so I walked her home. It had grown unusually cold out, well below freezing, and the hard Manhattan winds cut into us. Fortunately, we both had heavy, down, winter coats. Unfortunately, my coat was new and I could not get the zipper to zip up. I was trying to zip it up as we walked out of the pool hall, and struggled with it for about a block before giving up. After another block of walking into the wind like that I started to get *real* cold. I kept stopping, with my back turned to the wind, trying to zip the damn thing up, only to become quickly frustrated and continue along with my jacket still open. Then the cold would catch up to me again. It was really quite silly to watch, and had us both laughing about it, my own laughs not unmixed with pain.

"Here, stand still," Delia said, standing close in front of me and trying to figure out the zipper herself. "It's just, see you have to line these two up and ... Gosh, you must be freezing, aren't you freezing?"

"I'm cold, but I'm ok."

After a few minutes of trying, with her gloves off and fingers trembling in the cold, Delia couldn't get the zipper to work, either. It would have been a good opportunity to hold her hands, but I was too cold.

"See? It's not just that I'm a retard or something, it really is the zipper."

"Yeah."

"Thank you, Delia."

She blushed slightly in the glare of the street lights.

"Yeah, gosh, I just wish it would, it's just – you must be

so cold. Here, let's hurry so you can get into the subway."

I put my arm around her and squeezed her up against me. Delia caught her breath tensely, and drew back. So I let go after a moment and just chuckled, in what I hoped was a friendly way. We walked a little in silence, then she brought up some random subject or other we had been discussing earlier in the evening and our conversation took off again.

At Delia's building, she apologized again that she couldn't feed me or invite me inside. My face was so cold I could barely feel it. Both of our stomachs were growling over the wind. Delia still seemed so standoffish to me, in her body language, that I couldn't see kissing her good-night, not even a peck. And I was so cold and hungry that I didn't care anymore. We stood awkwardly at the bottom of the stairs for a few seconds.

I quickly kissed her on the cheek, and she ran up the stairs to her building as fast as she could, then rushed inside.

A text message signal sounded on my phone as I raced down the eery, empty street to the subway stairs, but I ignored it. Down the stairs, the subway platform meant warmth and shelter, even if I had to keep a wary watch on my surroundings.

Soon enough I was home and warm, devouring a massive, delicious meal. Probably ramen. Checking my phone, I had received a text message from Delia.

It said, "I had a really great time tonight, thank you!"

Which made me feel kind of nice, as I'd started to think the evening had been a disaster.

I can't remember what I texted back.

2/21

The following Saturday night we planned to have dinner at Rice. Not Spice. Delia met me at my apartment again, as it was on the way down to the restaurant. Around 8 p.m. She was a bit more dressed up and put together this time. Anyway, it was good to see her. I'd missed her in the intervening week.

"The thing is, a friend of mine is flying into town tonight, and she's staying with me. I just found out about it. She's great, but she's just spontaneous like that. So I'm going to have to go meet her when she calls me, probably around 10 or 11. I'm really sorry."

Um… Was she really sorry? I couldn't tell, really. At least she said it. I really didn't care. Didn't figure she was under any obligation to spend the whole night with me yet, anyway. Really.

"Hey, that's ok. Let's go have a nice dinner while we have a chance then."

"Great."

"Do you want to walk or take a cab?" I wondered. "I think we have time to walk, it's kind of nice out. Crisp. But, you have to go soon, so a cab will get us there faster."

"Yeah. No, I like to walk. It's only about 15 minutes' walk away, anyway. It would be good to get some fresh air."

I thought about looking at a map as we were heading out, just to be sure I knew where we were going. Just out of paranoia, because I don't have a great sense of direction. But I did know where we were going, and so did Delia, so I tried to relax and stop second guessing myself.

We walked south through Washington Square Park; it was nice. Not too many people out tonight, in the winter. Not hanging out, anyway. Always people out. See what I mean? It wasn't too cold, either, so that was good. I had mastered the zipper on my coat by now.

I talked to Delia about her writing. [She was a writer, did I tell you that?] She told me how she always smoked when she was writing, and now she was trying to give up smoking. It somehow made it hard to write – the habit change. I told her of a classical composer who had had the same problem.

I tried to tell her about my own writing, but she wasn't much interested. Didn't want to hear it. I get that a lot.

And, of course, the people who really are interested, and really want to see and know, they're kind of scary, aren't they? Like, why do they care? And you're afraid to show it to them. You'd rather be exposed to someone who doesn't, you know? Not really. It's like a tragedy, kind of.

Say Catch-22, but that's just an irony. It's not tragic, not really.

Sometimes digression is a tragedy…

Our conversation went so well that for a long time neither of us realized we were lost.

Then I saw the Brooklyn Bridge.

"Oh sh–no," I said. "It can't be this far. Shoot, I'm sorry, I've taken us the wrong way."

"It's ok."

"I feel like it's right around here somewhere."

"Yeah."

"Well you used to work down here; don't you know?" I suggested hopefully.

"I know how to get there from where I worked. I thought you knew the way. You're supposed to get us there, bud."

"Yeah, well I think if we just go down back this way

and turn right, we'll run right into it. I feel dumb to get a cab when we're just a few blocks away."

"Yeah."

It was starting to get pretty cold again.

I'm not sure how to describe the interim here, but imagine ninety minutes or more of walking through cold, windy streets. *Real* windy. And imagine you're pretty hungry, too. And imagine you're Delia, which means you're only about 5' tall and you're keeping pace with me at 6'. And imagine you're me, and you're engrossed in conversation with a pretty girl who is eager to talk and talk and talk, and you keep thinking your destination is just around the next corner down the road, and you keep getting there and finding out you were totally wrong, and then you turn the corner and see the Brooklyn Bridge in front of you again. Then you realize how long you have been walking! And imagine you look over and you notice that this pretty little girl chatting so eagerly next to you is cold, and tired, and hungry, and wasn't at all prepared for a long walk like this, and probably didn't even really want to walk in the first place. And while you're imagining that you could imagine that she isn't the only one who is exhausted, either, and that the few people on the streets here, as chance would have it, are totally sketchy and leering at both of you, and that you don't want to try to ask THEM for directions and admit you're lost, which could mean a mugging!

Ninety minutes after first "running into" the Brooklyn Bridge, we had traveled, at a fast walking pace, in an enormous, intricate, perverse, spirit sapping circle. Conversation finally died and we trudged on in silence.

I can't tell you that I felt like an idiot. That would be untrue. What I actually felt was shame. Pure, unadulterated.

I remembered how we thought up the idea to go to Rice in the first place. "Oh, I'm sorry. I didn't mean 'Spice,' I meant 'Rice'." I was kind of amazed that Delia was still walking with me. Or maybe she felt like she didn't have a choice.

Did you ever have that weird dream where everything is going wrong for no apparent reason and you're all mixed up and can't figure out what's happening. And everyone around you is just cool with it, like they don't seem to really care, and they like you and are nice to you and want to hang out with you even though you're the cause of all the problems. We've all had that dream, haven't we? Sure we have. Well, anyway, I was living that dream.

[That night, when I finally went to sleep, I dreamed that I got up in the morning, ate breakfast, brushed my teeth, talked to my parents on the phone, thought about going to church, and then went back to bed.]

"I'm really sorry," I said, "I feel like an idiot. At this point, even if we find the place, we probably don't have time to eat, since you have to go meet your friend. And Rice might not even still be open. I feel like I dragged you on this enormous wild good chase."

"It's ok. I think we still have time," Delia said saintfully. If that's a word. "Here, let's ask these people over here."

I collared the folks that Delia pointed to, who didn't actually look sketchy, and they immediately directed us to the restaurant, which was only a block away.

We were freezing, but Rice was still open. It felt good to get out of the cold. Really good.

"Wow, I can't believe we're finally here," one of us said.

"I know, I'm starving, let's get some food," said the other.

Rice was a cozy little restaurant that specialized in organic rice dishes, and hippy food in general. And, the surprising part: it was good.

One of those New York places just different enough to have a little bit of character. It was about the size of a small studio apartment, with a red, subdued lighting thing going on. Tables were crammed in along both walls; tall, standing tables on one side, small short tables against a bench on the other, with a narrow aisle down the middle.

I had gone here before with Nathalie. My first and only previous visit. The place conjured up some of my most treasured memories.

There was a tiny bathroom in the back, which even the unlikeliest New York establishments always somehow manage to squeeze in, and I excused myself to visit it. I knocked and tested the doorknob, then waited outside the door. For ten minutes I waited there anxiously, then gave up and started back to my seat (in pain). Catching sight of me, our waitress pointed out that the bathroom was, in fact, empty. All I needed to do was push hard to open the door. Really? But it was locked, I swear!

I spent about two minutes in there, hurrying because I had already been gone so long. It would have been nice to stand in front of the mirror for a few minutes and recompose myself. As I came out of the bathroom door, I tripped and hit my head on something, hard. It hurt a lot. Walking back to our table, I felt a bit shell-shocked, and laughed semi-hysterically under my breath while shaking my head.

"Are you alright?" Delia asked, with genuine concern in her voice.

"Yeah, I just..."

"What?"

"It's nothing."

"No, tell me."

"Sorry, just it seems like everything is going wrong tonight. I feel like some kind of buffoon. Like no matter what happens tonight I'm going to make a fool out of myself, and I already have. And I feel really bad for dragging you all around downtown New York in the dead of winter…"

I said something like that, but I don't think it was very coherent. Delia was sweet about it, though. I think she was just too hungry to reflect on the situation. Mutual starvation was becoming the cornerstone of our relationship.

"I ordered some edamame."

"Oh, ok," I said, "what's that?"

"Edamame?" she sounded confused.

"Yeah, what is it?"

"You don't know what edamame is?"

"Should I?"

The waitress brought over a bowl full of the stuff. It was good. She took our order while she was at it.

"What do you recommend that's vegan?" I asked, trying to sound serious and casual at the same time. Sort of like, "It's cool and everything, but it's important that you get this right."

Considering this was a sort of hippy joint, our waitress was strangely surprised by the question.

"Vegan?"

"Yeah, it has to be vegan, I'm extremely allergic to milk."

"Oh, well, yeah we have some vegan dishes. This one, 'Ginger Rice Medley' is vegan I think. It's really good."

"It *is* vegan?"

"Hold on. Jake! 'Ginger Rice Medley' is vegan, right?"

We heard an affirmative grunt from the direction of the

kitchen.

"Yeah, it's vegan, yeah, it's really good. That's what I recommend."

New York hippy is sort of 'faux' hippy. Not like where I'm from. To hippies, this stuff is supposed to be serious business!

Delia ordered something, too, and we began devouring the edamame in earnest. Pretty soon I felt the inside of my mouth start swelling up, so I stopped eating it. We relaxed a little and started talking again.

I'm not sure how we could have stumbled onto the subject, but Delia managed to express to me the great love she still felt for her ex-boyfriend.

"I really love him, you know?"

But, of course, I didn't know. In fact I had heard this from a girl before, and all I *knew* about it was that it did not bode well for me.

"You love your ex-boyfriend," I echoed her.

"Yeah, I really love him."

"So, he broke up with you?"

"No! No, no, he wanted us to stay together. He asked me to marry him. I'm just not ready for that, you know?"

Not really...

"I broke up with him," she continued, "because he was leaving the country and I couldn't deal with a long term relationship. And we'd been together so long, I kind of felt like I was losing myself."

"But if he was here, you guys would still be together."

"Well, yeah. Of course."

We talked about her and her boyfriend for a while, but that was all I got out of it. He was from Nicaragua or something. Somebody later told me the guy was a jackass, but I have no way of knowing if that's true.

The food was good. Sitting in this cozy little restaurant, eating delicious food, sort of put into perspective the adventure we just had.

"I can't believe how far we walked," Delia said in astonishment. "My feet hurt, I think I have blisters all over my feet."

I looked down and realized that, underneath the long hem of her pants, Delia was wearing some kind of fancy platform shoes, with a four or five inch sole. She seemed to be in genuine pain.

"Oh no," I said, "I feel horrible about that."

"And you almost got me hit by a car!"

"What? No I didn't. When?"

"Yes you did," she said emphatically, "You dragged me out in front of that car and his light was green; he almost ran me over."

Now she was looking at me with a sort of affectionate amazement, as if to say, "What the hell is wrong with you?"

"You didn't even notice that that guy almost ran us over?!?" she said, rubbing her feet.

"Well, there was that one guy, but he saw us, he wasn't going to hit us."

"He almost ran us over!!!"

We continued chatting and shoveling food into our mouths. It was delicious, probably the best vegan food I ever had. Not that there was anything fancy about it, just organic rice and vegetables and sauces and spices — somehow they whipped it together and it became sublime. I guess it helps if you're half-starving. Our spirits improved considerably.

Just when we were really getting into our food, and starting to finally enjoy ourselves, Delia's phone rang. She grimaced for my benefit as she answered it, but the result was inevitable – she had to leave. Soon.

"I'm really sorry," she said, resuming the litany about how crazy and unpredictable her friend was. How this was all beyond her control.

"It's ok," I said simply, and we tried to make the most of the next ten or fifteen minutes together.

Our conversation became easier again, lighter. I can't remember if I held her hand across the table, but hope I did. It would have been nice, for both of us. These were the best moments of the evening.

When we stepped back into the cold, Delia and I searched half-heartedly for a cab. We were both trying to delay, but was it for the same reason? I was looking for a graceful moment to kiss her. Maybe Delia was thinking the same thing, but she walked ahead of me, or to the side of me but yards away. Talking, delaying, but always directing a lot of negative, defensive body language towards me. I was too insecure to overcome it.

We walked together for a block or two, letting a handful of taxis pass. Finally it was getting really cold again, and Delia already risked being late to help her friend. We stood on the curb and hailed the next cab coming towards us from the distance.

"Oh, shit, a mini-van cab!" Delia exclaimed, and leapt back from the curb as it came closer into view. "I hate mini-van cabs. Oh no, I hope he doesn't stop."

The cabby, apparently accustomed to this sort of behavior, had already spotted us, and pulled up assertively alongside. Without turning back around, Delia began to get in.

"Delia." I said in gentle accusation, touching her shoulder, drawing her back from the cab.

"Oh my gosh! I'm sorry."

She looked startled, but was smiling as she quickly stepped back onto the curb and embraced me tightly. I kissed her cheek, which was the only part of her face I could get to without resorting to force. Then the cab was speeding away. As it faded down the street, Delia sat up against the back window waving, and beaming at me.

2/24

I was wandering the streets of Manhattan with some friends…

The wind bit into us; we walked quickly, but talked lightly.

"So, Killah," a friend of a friend of mine began, resting a conspiratorial hand on my shoulder. "What's the situation with you and Kieran's friend, Delia?"

"Well, we've gone out a couple times. I saw her on Saturday, actually."

"And?"

I stepped over the gutter as our group moved to cross an intersection. Skimmed my eyes across the cold white lines painted on the black street; the bright green and red shine of the traffic; blurry yellow cabs flashing by, damp, reflecting the millions and millions of lights dimly, brilliantly diffusing their energy into the city.

"And?" I reversed the question.

"Did you stick it in her butt?"

"Aw, get out of here, man."

"What?" he feigned innocence.

"You know, it's weird, though, it's like she's sending me all these mixed signals."

"What do you mean?"

"I don't know, just her body language, and the way she acts towards me. Physically, it's like she's just not giving me any openings."

Someone up ahead shouted. The various members of our group, caught up in their own conversations, jogged forward, or quickened their pace, or laughed.

"Come on, guys!" someone called.

"Killah, she's gone out with you two weekends in a row. How much opening do you need?"

Good point.

2/28

Saturday again. Delia and I were planning to see each other, but we had not made any definite arrangements. I got ahold of her on the phone late that morning.

"Hey, Delia, how you doing?"

"Good. How are you this morning?"

"Not too bad. I actually got up this morning and did some laundry-"

"Me too!"

"Hehe, yeah? And I went and bought some groceries."

"Same. And I did some dishes."

"Dishes, yeah I did dishes. I guess we're on the same wavelength today, eh. So listen, I had a few ideas about tonight-"

"You know what," she said quickly, breaking in, "actually, a friend of mine's playing a concert downtown tonight."

"Downtown?"

"Yeah, he's this really great guy, one of my best friends. He was practically like a father to me when I was waitressing at Johnson's. He's a bartender there. So, anyway, a bunch of us are going to go down and watch tonight. Why don't you come with us?"

So I ended up heading down to the financial district to meet up with Delia and her friends. It seemed kind of a strange place for a concert, down near the World Trade Center ruins. The financial district down there had never had a lot of night life, and after 9/11 that little bit immediately dried up. It was hard to find so much as an open bar in the vicinity of the WTC. A concert down there was thus an intriguing prospect. I had an address, and the name of the establishment; I looked on the event as a little bit of an adventure. *Frank's Roadhouse Bar & Grill* – the name sounded so mocking, so ironic. New York, in a mixed up sort of way.

That night I caught a train downtown, and walked over to West Broadway where the place was supposed to be. Couldn't find it. I walked around for a while. Tried to call Delia, but couldn't get ahold of her. Amazingly, there was a different club open on the block, though they didn't seem to have many patrons, so I asked the bouncer out front if he knew where it was.

"Frank's Roadhouse Bar & Grill?" he laughed, "Never heard of it."

I walked down the road. I knew I had the street right, but maybe I had mis-copied the address? Or maybe *Frank's Roadhouse Bar & Grill* in downtown Manhattan didn't exist at all. Maybe this was some kind of big joke at my expense. I tried to call Delia again, couldn't reach her. Thought about going home. Kept walking.

I finally found it a couple of blocks farther down.

The tacky neon sign out front, which would have been at home on the side of any lonely highway in America, foreshadowed the rest of the evening. Stepping in, an old worn out bar faced the entrance, with a bunch of random junk decor scattered around, sports and contemporary Americana mementos pinned to the wall, and an old, broken, dusty jukebox in the corner. Past the bar, the room opened onto a dis-organized array of tables, benches, and chairs. Pressed up flush against this dining area was a three foot high stage just big enough for a small band. A conspicuous absence of chicken wire screened the stage.

The stage was the first thing I had noticed, really, when I got inside, because a man was up there screaming and tearing at a guitar. He was hard to miss: a carelessly dressed, bestubbled faced, forty year old, bald man screaming incoherently into the microphone while thrashing vigorously, yet somehow impotently, at his maximally amped instrument. A drummer and bassist were up there, too, although one didn't notice them much. It was the front man who really stood out. Literally, and figuratively. I stared open mouthed, stunned by the display. My ears slowly adjusted and began to filter through the aggressive wall of noise. I picked out a lyric or bit of melody here and there – they were trying to play covers of classic rock songs!

The band was just so incredibly bad, it was amazing. It was like if you took the worst high school garage band ever, like if you went and did a massive nationwide search to find them, leaving no stone in the country unturned, and then if you took them and you didn't let them communicate or talk to each other or practice their instruments for about twenty years. Then took their front man and had him team up with the sons of his two former band members, having been taught to play by their fathers, and without any practicing, just stuck them all up on a stage one night and told them to go crazy. Except it was worse than that! Because that might have been cool.

After a good long while, my eyes wandered down to the tables in the dining area. A whole lot of people were sitting down there eating. Drinking, laughing, talking, or trying to - their backs turned as much as possible to the cover band hovering above, screaming in their faces. The customers here were fatter and less attractive than what you normally find in New York. Steak and mashed potatoes seemed to be the preferred entrée, and a lot of them were really chowing down. I guess they were more easygoing than the usual New York crowd, too, because nobody seemed very upset about the wall of noise, despite the fact that most were conspicuously trying to ignore it and a few even openly mocking the band. For the most part, they seemed to be continuing with their drinks and dinners as if the band weren't even there at all. Like it was a ghost band.

After acclimating myself to this new environment, I scanned the tables and spotted Delia. She was sitting in the middle of one of the benches at a table in the back. A bunch of friends were sitting around her, drinking and laughing, watching the band. A few of these seemed to be the only ones really enjoying the performance and would shout encouragement in between numbers. I walked to the table and caught Delia's eye.

"Oh, hey!" she said, looking up without smiling, as if she were surprised to see me.

Everyone in the group turned to stare at me a moment,

and I slid into the (thankfully) empty space on the bench next to Delia, trying awfully hard to act confident and nonchalant. As the staring continued, I leaned over to kiss Delia on the cheek, but she leaned away and said something to the person next to her, laughing. So I just sort of squeezed her arm affectionately and allowed myself a wry grin. Our audience relaxed, and Delia leaned back over to talk to me.

"How's it going" she asked.

"Good. Good. How about you, did you have a good day?"

"Oh my gosh, I had the most incredible day today! It was the best day I've had in a really long time."

"Wow, that's awesome, what happened?"

Delia didn't say anything.

I smiled easily at her, trying to release the social tension in my body. The band, which had been setting up for a new number, started again in the background, noisily filling up the pause in our conversation.

"Well, what happened that was so awesome?" I asked again, shouting.

"I can't tell you," she shouted back matter of factly.

"What?"

"I can't tell you about it, it's sort of a secret."

This left me nonplussed. I sat silent for a moment, considering. Gave Delia a quizzical look. A subtle creep of guilt passed over her face. It still didn't make any sense.

"Well what did you do today?" she rejoined, smiling.

Plugging one of my ears to block out some of the noise, I leaned over, resting my left hand affectionately between Delia's neck and shoulder, so that I could speak directly into her ear and not have to shout.

"What, my day?" I said sarcastically, "It's all top secret and classified, you know. But don't worry, it was great. I hate to say it, but it's one of those things like in the movies where I could tell you, but then I'd have to kill you."

"You don't understand," she sighed.

"What, you had a hot date or something? I don't understand. What's the big deal?"

"It's nothing like that. I just had a really great day, that's all. It's not something I have to tell you about."

"What?"

"It's not something I have to tell you about! Just, let's talk about something else, ok. I wish I hadn't said anything at all."

"Well of course you don't HAVE to tell me about it. It's just a bit strange, that's all. Look, I'm sorry. Well, how long have you guys been here…"

We continued talking for a while, and gradually I got a picture of what Delia had done that day. There was some sort of secret society of super-rich people that her parents were a part of [Delia's father owned a large company], and Delia had finally gone to her first meeting with the New York chapter. Apparently, the people there were really amazing, and it was nice to finally have some folks to talk to who understood how difficult life could be for the super-rich. Not having friends who could relate to them, feeling isolated by their superior status, that sort of thing. Delia wasn't supposed to talk about it at all. It sounded a bit sordid, to be honest.

Noise from the band kept interrupting our conversation, so we spent a lot of time just sitting, watching them. Delia seemed genuinely impressed by the performance and expected me to feel the same way. But they were well below the standard at which I could feign admiration.

I mean, it was weird to sit in this restaurant with this old man right out in everyone's lap screaming maniacally

and a whole bunch of fat people sitting in front of him trying to ignore it. Chowing down turkey and mashed potatoes
like it's TGIFriday's or some shit. I've lived in small towns
in Oregon and Idaho, but I've never experienced that
before. Then Delia kept turning to me with this dreamy
look in her eyes,

"I think he's brilliant," she said, again and again.

Brilliant? Luckily the music was loud enough to excuse
me from any mandatory response. I think whenever she
said this I kind of nodded my head and turned away. The
volume of the band's performance made any subtle
response impossible, there was no room for verbal hedging.
Otherwise I might have said it was interesting, or different,
or that he had a lot of energy – or something like that. Or I
might have said it's terrible, I'm not sure. Didn't have to go
there.

And I hate to be so negative. Really, I apologize for
that. Looking back on it now, it actually could have been a
lot of fun, such a random experience and absurd. With the
right company it would have been. But I was already emotionally invested in my relationship with Delia, and trying to
work out how to move forward with that. Here I was with
her and all her friends, expected to enjoy this ridiculous
spectacle that the others seemed to take quite seriously,
while everyone watched and evaluated me – it made me
tense.

This didn't help: there was a cute little 22 year old girl
who Delia described as one of her best friends, and "like a
sister." She was wearing plastic, red, glittery hot pants and
running around hyperactively. Seemed really charged up. So
that's cool and everything, the weird part was when Delia
told me that her cute friend and the lead singer of the band
were a couple.

"I set them up," Delia said smugly.

"You did?"

"Yeah, when I was working at Johnson's, I was the one who introduced the two of them. And now they're, like, the perfect couple."

"Ah…"

"It's great, right? I just knew that they would be perfect for each other."

"…uh……"

Something interrupted our conversation at this point. Probably one of Delia's friends grabbed her and they went out to have a smoke. I was actively disinvited from these smoke rendezvous for some reason. The band was taking a break and I chatted with some of Delia's friends at the table; they seemed alright.

When the band finally finished their set our little group applauded, and everyone else went on slurping their mashed potatoes. Delia's friend Lacey, in the hot pants, ran over and embraced and kissed the lead singer, who I now learned was named Jerry. It was pretty fucked up, because he really looked like her father, and she really seemed to be turned on. Big time. Delia gave him a pretty intimate embrace as well, and he kissed her on the temple and then on the cheek. We all moved outside.

Everyone stood around in a little circle and congratulated the band members, telling them what a great job they did. Which is just the way, isn't it. Someone will go up, drop their drawers, and take a shit on stage, and at least 33% of the audience will congratulate them on giving such an awesome performance. I often wonder if people are just comfortable being disingenuous, even though deep down they *know* the performance was shit, or if there really is this large percentage of human beings who are incapable of any sort of discernment whatsoever.

Lacey was going wild.

"Oh my God, let me see your fingers, let me see your fingers! Do they have that black on them from the guitar strings, like oh, there it is, there it is! I love that! Like you've really been playing that guitar so hard, up on stage, oh my God! I love you! You rocked so hard! Oh my God!" She clutched at his fingers, effusing hysterically.

Jerry rested his other hand squarely on her ass, and gave an occasional nudge and a wink to one of his white haired, bespectacled friends.

"Hi Jerry, great show. So, this is your girlfriend Lacey."

"Lacey, I want you to meet my good friend William, we went to high school together."

It was just so messed up, these old white haired guys in pouchy old man jeans, goggling at this little girl and winking at each other. Delia beamed at Jerry and his friends, and I could only wonder what she was thinking. I mean, I'm not exaggerating at all, these guys were literally nudging and winking at each other, and occasionally some of Jerry's friends would look at Lacey and tell each other a joke and then laugh and stare at her ass and give Jerry a knowing grin. The younger guys, Delia's other friends, didn't act like that. It left me feeling dirty to be a part of the group.

We went back inside and Delia and I sat and worked on some of the games from one of those paper children's placemats with word puzzles and mazes and stuff on them. Together we failed to rearrange the letters e-r-o-n-a-g into the word o-r-a-n-g-e, but we got most of the other puzzles pretty quickly. I beat her three times in a row at tick tack toe, which I have to attribute to her drinking, because Delia was an intelligent girl. Or maybe she never realized that tick-tack-toe is a very simple game with only one way to win and you should always pick the center square first. Somehow we started talking about singing, and Delia commented that she sings in the shower.

"What do you sing?" I asked.

"Oh, you know, stupid little things from grade school and stuff."

"Like what? Sing something for me."

"…Fifty Nifty United States," she said, laughing.

"You sing Fifty Nifty? Really? That's awesome. We did that play when I was in 5th Grade. I was George Washington!" I said proudly.

"What play?" she asked.

"What? Oh, it was a play, you know, the song comes from a play about the Declaration of Independence or something. George Washington was the star role."

"Oh. That's cool, no, we just sang the song."

"How does it go again," I said, humming a few of the bars. "I can't remember."

"No, no, I only sing in the shower. I'm a terrible singer."

"I'm sure you're not terrible. That's a pretty strong word."

"It's embarrassing," she re-iterated.

"Oh, come on. Help me out here. I can't remember how the tune goes. Alabama… Alaska…"

"No."

"Oh, wait, I almost got it, 'Alabama.. Alaska,'" I started to pick the tune out lyric by lyric.

"No, stop ok?"

"Why?"

"If you start singing it," she said, "then I'm going to start singing along with you, because I can't help myself, and then it's going to be embarrassing. Please, don't."

I don't know whether she meant for it to or not, but that brought out a bit of the devil in me.

"Here, I'm sure you sing great, let's do it," and I broke into song.

"Alabama, Alaska, Arizona, Arkansas," then Delia joined in, and she really sounded just fine, although her voice quivered a little bit from nerves.

"California, Colorado, Connecticut," we continued, and a few bemused faces turned in our direction.

Somewhere around Iowa I started to mix the words up, and Delia laughed and corrected me, until we finished. Easily the high point of the night.

"See, that was great," I said, "you sound good, you hit all the notes, you don't sound terrible at all."

"Thanks. You're terrible," she said, smiling at me.

"Aww.."

Delia was starting to get this strange look on her face, though. Lacey came over and they whispered together. It wasn't late, only 11:30 or so, and I had only been there maybe an hour and a half, but the bar was already clearing out.

"Is everybody leaving?" I asked. "Do you want to go somewhere else?"

"Yeah, Justin, actually I think I'm going to go home. I'm don't feel very well."

Delia looked a little bit green in the face, so I could believe it, but she also acted sort of sheepish, like this was just an excuse to get away.

"Oh no, are you ok? What's wrong?"

"Yeah, actually I think I ate some bad shrimp earlier."

"Ah, uh oh, that's awful. Darn I was hoping we could maybe go somewhere else tonight, have a better chance to spend some time alone together."

We moved outside where Lacey was already hailing a cab. For the first time in the evening I got a chance to talk to Delia alone. I had the feeling that if I ever wanted to see her again I had to do something. But she was so distant from me emotionally, it's not like I could grab her and kiss her. Maybe I had some other chances to do that and missed them. Now she was cagier than ever. She stood at least four feet away from me while we talked, backing up every time I stepped forward.

"Do I make you nervous?" Delia asked, in a tone of voice that betrayed some feeling of insecurity, and made me feel kind of bad, like I'd done wrong by her somehow.

"No. You don't make me nervous. No, not at all. Listen, Delia..."

"Yeah?"

"I really like you, I mean, you're a sweet girl, and you're smart, and you're pretty. I mean, I'm really attracted to you. But I feel bad, because I feel like I haven't really had a chance to show you how I feel."

"Yeah...."

"It just seems like you're kind of preempting me, sort of drawing away whenever I move forward."

"Well, I think that's because I am," she said softly.

A cab pulled up and started honking. Lacey swung the door open and screamed for Delia to get in.

"Oh, no, this is terrible," Delia said, looking at the cab. "The thing is, I mean," she continued more quickly, "you're great, you have a great personality, and you're good looking, and you're really smart; I really enjoy being with you, but, like, I just can't get into a relationship right now. I mean, I want us to go out together and enjoy each other, I just don't want to worry about any kind of commitment or relation-ship, but — yeah, just to have a good time and enjoy ourselves."

The cabby honked some more.

"Enjoy each other, you mean physically too?" I said, cutting to the chase.

"Well, yeah, of course. Look, this is terrible, I really have to go. We need to finish this conversation; I'll call you tomorrow, ok?"

"No, that's ok," I said, "that sounds ok. Call me tomorrow, and I hope you feel better!"

Delia hugged me quickly, jumped into the cab, and it sped away.

I decided to walk home and think about things. Down there at night, in the shadows of those huge buildings in the financial district, it can be so peaceful. Even along Broadway. You are surrounded by humanity, the work of human hands, but stunningly alone. Wrapped in peculiar tranquility. You feel close to your thoughts, which rise easily with the lines of the skyscrapers around you. The lights everywhere, piercing through and tattering the darkness, seem to illuminate darknesses of your own. Like being alone in the far off wilderness, and surrounded by people at the same time. Like just for an evening you can become a ghost, and pass silently over the world. And feel it and experience it without touching or being touched by it. And without losing your connection to humanity. When you can reflect. This was what drew me to New York in the first place, I came here to find it. A hint of something seen in movies and on TV, something that I believed in.

I love to walk by myself through the city. To pass under the tall buildings, tread lightly over the concrete, and maybe sit down here or there. Feel the gaze of the millions of people not on me, and, in the midst of all that human energy, be wrapped up and alone with my thoughts. I love to walk solitary at night when I get a chance.

Delia loomed over my mind like one of those great buildings. I thought a lot about her, and about me. I didn't know if I really wanted a 'no strings attached' relationship. What I wanted was a wife, a soul-mate. Sex without love seemed like such a waste. Sullying. I was still pretty much the idealist. Still holding onto that dream of true love, marriage, family. Should have known better by then. Nowadays I just hope I'll be able to have a few *illegitimate* children. Maybe poke some holes in a condom or something.

"Oops."
"Haha, oops what?"
"Umm…"
"Oh, shit, did you –"
"It ripped."

Or something like that, I guess. I dunno. I hadn't yet become so disillusioned. On the other hand, I was awfully lonely. And your sex drive beats the hell out of you if you try to ignore it, doesn't it. Fuck, I knew that better than anyone. And women don't like you as much if you don't bring the requisite experience to the table. That's a hard kind of self-reinforcing lesson I had already guessed at. Just a casual relationship could be good for me in a lot of ways.

I didn't reach any conclusion, but walked all the way home and went to sleep.

CHAPTER 9

Eve came and went often after that. Always happily, always welcome and sorry to leave. She always had work she was missing in the forest. She had to be back in Atlantis for market day, and her family would worry about her.

At the strangest times, she would appear. Once late at night, just as Adam was falling asleep. A whisper came from the window.

"Adam. Adam, are you awake?"

"Eve?"

She didn't want anything in particular, just to see him, to talk for a little while. She wouldn't even let him kiss her, not even on the cheek, or take her hand. Then she disappeared as quickly again, into the night, to sleep among the trees.

One morning Adam woke early to find Eve asleep outside his door. She was huddled up against the wall of the tower, shivering unconsciously against the cold stone.

"Eve?"

She woke instantly, as Adam knelt to touch her. Proceeding, nevertheless, he squeezed her gently, filled with concern.

"Eve?"

"Adam!"

She hugged him tightly to her.

"Eve, what's wrong? Why are you asleep out here?"

"What? Nothing's wrong. I wanted to see you first thing in the morning."

"You're freezing. Come inside, I'll get the fire up."

Adam half carried her inside.

"I'm alright," Eve giggled, clinging affectionately to his neck.

"Why did you want to see me?"

"Why? I like seeing you, that's why. There's no reason. How is your garden coming along?"

"No reason?"

"No reason."

"Everything's alright?"

"Everything," Eve said, staring solemnly into his eyes, not allowing them to stray from her.

He breathed a sigh of relief.

"The garden— Well, the garden is growing beautifully. Almost magically. Did you notice outside, the grains are already sprouting."

"I saw that."

"I've decided to christen it 'New York'. Not just the garden, but this whole deserted city. My home away from home."

Adam paused, meaningfully, and held his breath.

"Is it ok?" he asked gravely, as if the question were deeply important and the answer in doubt.

"You don't need my permission," Eve said.

"I know, but, you were here before me, and I want it. And I trust your judgment."

"I think it's a beautiful name."

This time they did kiss. And Adam got very little work done that day, although Eve left again late the same morning.

Standing in the fields, he lost himself in thought. Dreaming of Eve, but not only of her. Of all the new ideas that she had brought into his life, that this whole planting experience had brought to him. He thought about York and his life there, and why things were the way they were. Gradually, sometimes shockingly, or almost imperceptibly, Adam thought about how things could be different.

Nothing had been different in York for thousands of years. The very concept of change had died out long ago. True, the seasons changed, and the stars in the sky canted about their peculiar mechanisms, but these were the patterns of life and repeated themselves uniformly. The lives of the people in York had always repeated themselves. Change was not simply unheard of, it was a concept they could scarcely comprehend.

As week passed into week, Adam began to wrap his mind around it: the inexorably new.

"There is a difference between Eve and I," he thought to himself. "Something deep, something seated in the way we understand... things. Eve is, so–. So–. She's so insecure."

No one in York was insecure. Why would they be? How could they be? Each person had their own place, played their own part in the community. As their parents had before them. Everyone had a garden, an old stone house, and apple trees.

Eve's world was different. Adam did not quite understand how.

"If Eve is a real woman," he thought, "and she is young, and she is waiting to be matched, then she could be matched with me. And if Eve were matched with me, then I would marry a woman who was not from York. Not from York – it's so strange. And if I married a woman who was not from York then a young woman from York would not have anyone to marry. Eve would come to York, and York...

"York would be as it had never been before. It would be new. It would be, not new like a fresh sprouting plant, but new like a plant which appears from nowhere, the kind of which no one has seen before. New, like Eve.

"Except Eve is a young woman just as any I have known. But not the same."

In this way Adam tumbled through his thoughts, reshaping, polishing, and refining his understanding of the world. Often obsessively, without conscious volition. Conclusions seemed to lie perpetually outside his grasp, but the outlines of their forms emerged.

Before he was sure of anything else, Adam was sure of one thing: he should be matched with Eve. This he knew, understood completely. He felt it. A visceral, emotional knowledge of self, quite beyond reason's scope.

rhapsody for electric guitar, bass, drum set, and small kazoo.

This story is fast paced and involves drunkenness but only minimal amounts of debauchery. Appetite whetted?   No? Damn.

Well, ok, it involves this awesome rock band and stuff. How about now? No?

Um.... well, there is a girl in a wet tank top, and her breasts are pretty big by the way....

Yes? - No?

That part isn't very much of it, though. You can forget that. Forget I said that. Appealing to the lowest common denominator and whatever. Bait and switch. I apologize. It's not that kind of a story.

It has people trying to intimidate others and then getting accused of being gay. ...Maybe?

Try it out. Adam and Eve will be back shortly.

I'M ABOUT TO GO to sleep early on a Friday night. Feeling a bit depressed, to be honest. Then my friend Jack calls and says he is thinking about going out to some rock concert. He hasn't heard the band in years, but "they used to be good." I'm not such a big hard rock fan, but, fuck it, it's better than going to bed early, lonely and depressed on a Friday night.

"Cool, let's do it," I say decisively into the phone.

Jack lives in the same building as me. We meet in the lobby half an hour later and walk quickly to catch the train. In New York they call subway cars trains. That's because they are. Trains, that is. Anyways, another friend, Kevin, meets us there.

We are in Greenwich Village and we're trying to get far-ther downtown to Tribeca, an odd place to find a rock club these days, but nevertheless. We catch a train heading downtown, which should get us there right away. The ride starts to seem like it is taking a long time. Our train emerges out of the ground onto a bridge and we are crossing the East River into Brooklyn.

"Umm... guys, are we supposed to be crossing the river?" I enquire rhetorically to my friends, who are lost in conversation.

"What?"

"Oh, shit."

"It's cool, it's cool, it's cool," Jack says rapidly, "we'll just catch the train back at the first station." Then he says, "shit," despondently for good measure.

Some of the other passengers on the train laugh at us, but not in an unfriendly way, and not too much either because I'm looking at them. Otherwise the train ride is pretty boring, isn't it?

Soon enough we are in Tribeca, looking for the Tribeca Rock Club. None of us really know the neighborhood (does anyone?), but we find the Rock Club quickly enough. $10 at the door, not bad for a concert in Manhattan.

Inside the club, an opening band is playing and the crowd is still pretty small. Jack insists on staking out "good seats", which is cool. The walls are lined with some sort of tiered bench platform bleacher things, so we establish a position on one of these and Kevin goes and buys some drinks at the bar, but I'm not drinking yet.

This pretty blonde girl comes and stands next to us. Cool. She's accompanied by an older, nervous looking woman (mother? sister? co-worker?) and seems really hopped up for the event. I overhear something about how she has been wanting to see the band all her life and that they drove a long way to get here.

The band is called "Local H", by the way.

Local H is a singer/guitar and drums power duo. The singer-guitarist, the front man, walks onto the stage carrying a whiskey bottle and drinks heavily from it before picking up a guitar. He fiddles with some big flash-lamp things that are pointed at the audience and seem out of place. He says a few words to the audience, then someone shouts out, "Bound For The Floor!", then he says, "Fuck you, mother-fucker!" and starts playing.

The music is incredible, I can't believe what I'm hearing. Somehow the guy plays guitar and bass lines at the same time, and it sounds like a full band. He also improvises a lot as he goes, but without losing the melodic line.

A mosh pit forms, and everyone starts screaming, "And fuck New York too!" along to the music. It sounds quaint, but *is* awesome. The men in the mosh pit begin crashing into more timid souls occupying the first level of bleachers.

Some of the women on the bleachers cower, while their male companions make a show of pushing intruders roughly back into the fray. Or as roughly as they are able and think they can get away with. Our group is on the second level, so we're unaffected, but just below us the nervous companion of the pretty blonde girl is being crashed into constantly, and looks discomposed by it. Tempted to dive into the mosh pit myself, I offer to trade places with her between songs. She accepts gratefully. True, I have an ulterior motive, but I would have taken pity on her anyway. A bunch of yobs jumping around spastically is no big deal to me. Anyways, now I'm standing next to the pretty blonde girl, which was the goal, and I try to chat her up a little whenever it is quiet enough. She seems nice.

The concert continues frenetically and each song is better than the last. The singer drinks more and more out of the whiskey bottle, sometimes while playing. If anyone thought that was just for show, it quickly becomes apparent that he is getting very literally wasted. But the music doesn't seem to suffer, it just becomes more intense.

We are in a pretty small room; a long, narrow brick box that can't hold more than perhaps 300 people. I think it said on the wall that their legal capacity is 250. You have a sense that if a fire breaks out you're definitely going to die.

So we're all standing in this dark, brick hall, wiling out, enjoying the concert, and all of a sudden the whiskey-guitar man pulls a cord that sets off the flash lamps he was fiddling with earlier. There is a collective groan. I see white for a few seconds, and my eyes hurt a lot.

"Ow, that's not cool," I shout, to no one in particular.

Local H plays on as if nothing happened and we all start enjoying the concert again, pulled by the intense vibe. After a few minutes, whiskey-guitar pulls the cord to set the lamps off again, and it hurts again. The third time we are more prepared.

The best solution is to look away just before the flash-lamps go off, then the whole audience lights up brighter than day and you can get in some real interesting people watching. Most aren't keyed into this strategy, however, and it is difficult to time it right. A few people are drunk enough not to care already, but most just grit their teeth when the lamps go off and try to ride it out. Whiskey-guitar becomes more and more drunk, and the more drunk he becomes, the more he seems to relish pulling the little cord and shooting these damn stadium flash lamps off in our faces. It's starting to piss people off. But the music is awesome and most of the audience members seem like big fans of the band.

They keep playing, and if they would just stop flashing the lamps it might be the best concert ever. It's hard and fast, but not too much, just kind of honest, and with really good melodic lines running throughout, holding everything together. Sort of a melodic synthesis of metal, punk, alt, and good, old fashioned, rock.

The band winds up to its finale, at the end of which whiskey-guitar stands there shooting the flash lamps at us over and over and over again, until the audience, even while trying to be "hard core" and "into it", begins to take on a "troubled, worried" air. All of our eyes hurt from the flashes, and whiskey-guitar looks wobbly, like he's not 100% sure how to stand up anymore, or walk.

With a bit of stumbling, then, they wander off the stage. Of course we scream for an encore. The flash lamps seem to be used up, at least. They come back out after a good, long while. Whiskey-guitar looks really blasted now. His face is grey, and a tremor plays across his cheek. The drummer, by contrast, is completely sober, some cross between bored and horrified.

Whiskey starts flailing wildly away at his guitar, belting out a song that nobody seems to have heard before. It sounds pretty cool – edgy. More edgy than cool. As the song goes on he seems like he's just making up the words. It doesn't appear to have a proper end, but finally boils itself down to one line, sung over and over again: "Fuck Jamie Newell!"

No one seems to know who Jamie Newell is, although some are trying to make out the name and sing along.

After a few minutes of this repetition the drummer stands up and walks off stage. Whiskey-guitar looks around, confused, then sets his instrument on the stage and walks over to the drum set. He picks up two errant drum sticks, and, clutching them in his fist like weapons, begins slamming them down violently into the snare, in a kind of chanting rhythm.

"Fuck Jamie Newell! Fuck Jamie Newell!" he screams hoarsely, and most of the audience joins in, laughing at the joke.

After a few minutes, though, audience participation dies off and he is left alone on the stage with his bottle of whiskey and bizarre, angry chant. Which doesn't seem to bother him at all, as he continues for another five minutes before, mercifully, one of the drumsticks breaks. Whiskey-guitar stares confusedly at the broken stick, hurls it into the audience, picks up what's left of his bottle of whiskey, and walks backstage.

"Wow," I comment, as full lights come up and everyone starts heading for the door.

"Awesome concert, man," Jack says enthusiastically, "That was raw!"

"Yeah, that was pretty cool," Kevin says, "I liked it."

"Let's get out of here and go find a bar," Jack says.

"Yeah," Kevin says, "the bar here kind of sucks."

I hang back and chat with the blonde girl and her friend for a minute. They seem to have had a good time. I ask her if they would like to come have a drink with us, but she declines. Sensing my window of opportunity slamming shut, I awkwardly attempt to execute one of the "moves" that I have learned from the Internet.

"Well, I'm really sorry I'll... never..see you again," I force myself to say.

She looks at me with a vaguely indecipherable expression.

"Yeah," she says simply, then tries to turn away, and I walk quickly back to the door as my face burns.

I catch up with Jack and Kevin outside, and they wonder what has been holding me up.

"I wanted to talk to that blonde girl who was standing next to us," I say exasperatedly.

"Yeah, that was a cute girl, man, you should have asked her to come have a drink with us," Jack says.

"I did."

"Oh, no dice?"

"Nope."

"Maybe she's underage, man."

"You think?"

"That girl looks pretty young, man, maybe you could get her to come have coffee with us or something."

It's a good idea, but, I conclude that my chances are already shot to shit, so we move on. It's about midnight and the concert has left the three of us with energy to burn.

"I think that's my favorite band now," I say sincerely as the buzz of rock and roll continues looping through my veins.

"That concert was dope, man!" Jack agrees. "Dude, I know the best place for us to go. The Village Idiot! It's perfect!"

"I don't know if I can do that tonight, guys," Kevin says warily.

"What's The Village Idiot?" I ask.

"Dude, you can do it. Dude, The Idiot is this insane bar up on 14th St. It's legend! Last time I went to The Idiot one of their hot bartender girls grabbed me and we hooked up on top of the bar. The Idiot is the bar that Coyote Ugly was based on, man, every time you go there it's insane. Totally insane."

"I don't know, guys," Kevin says, "The Idiot, that's — you have to be in the right mood for that."

"Let's do it!" I say, so we catch a cab up to 14th.

Outside the bar there are a bunch of sailors milling around, miscellaneous party girls, two random, dirty, long haired guys screaming at each other. There are sailors all over the neighborhood. Apparently, it's fleet week.

"This is The Idiot, man," Jack says with satisfaction.

We stand outside for a little while and take in the scene while Jack and Kevin "smoke a butt". The long haired guys screaming at each other accept a truce negotiated by their friends. Some of the sailors move inside, others walk on down the street, and more people come out of the bar to have a smoke, filling in empty spaces on the sidewalk. The Idiot doesn't have any windows, just a big wooden door with an ancient red and white wooden placard nailed into the bricks above it, reading: "The Village Idiot". It seems out of place beside the shiny new nightclubs up and down the street.

I'm not a smoker and it's making me uneasy just standing around outside without much of any idea what lies within. It's more than that that's bothering me, though. It's Jack and Kevin's attitude about the place. A sense of anticipation in the air. Like, just inside the door lies some great adventure and they can taste it on their lips. Not only anticipation, but apprehension, a vague sense of danger. That sense you get when the adrenaline of people around you is rising and you're not sure why.

We pull back the wooden doors and maneuver our way through the people crowding the entrance. The bar is brightly lit and packed body to body, an irreducible morass of shouting, drinking, dancing. Peculiarly, there is no bouncer at the door, or anywhere to be seen. There must be one around, though. At least, one would hope. Music is pumped throughout the bar at a truly overwhelming volume, maybe even louder than the rock concert and without the breaks between numbers. Screaming and sign language become the only available means of communication.

A long, wooden bar fronts up against the entranceway. Down past the bar, if you can squeeze through the crush, there is a big open room scattered with small tables, chairs, and a dart board. Hung on the wall behind the bar are hundreds of pairs of bras and panties. The bar itself is staffed by six or seven cute-ish, young-ish women in jean shorts and miniskirts. They are working furiously, frantically, literally running up and down the bar from customer to customer, yet still find time for a laugh here, a smile there, or a quick little, butt shaking dance. It keeps the atmosphere sharp, and happy. And wild.

We slowly, over the course of ten or fifteen minutes, squeeze up against the bar to get some drinks.

"WATCH THIS, DUDE," Jack says knowingly, and orders a round of tequila shots.

The girl brings us six instead of three, and only charges us three dollars. Normally, a single shot of tequila in a Manhattan bar would run at least five. I try to tell her about the mistake, but she's already gone, throwing drinks onto the bar for another customer.

"I TOLD YOU, I TOLD YOU," Jack exclaims happily, "IT'S NOT A MISTAKE, MAN, THAT'S THE WAY THEY DO IT HERE."

Kevin shies away from the tequila.

"I DON'T KNOW, I CAN'T DRINK TEQUILA TONIGHT. I NEED A BEER."

"OH, OK, OK, MAN, IT'S COOL."

One of us orders a couple of Coronas. A different girl slams three Coronas down on the bar and opens them.

"WAIT! WE ONLY ORDERED TWO," I say.

She smiles knowingly and passes all three of them to us.

"ONE DOLLAR EACH, TWO DOLLARS TOTAL," she screams, winks at us, grabs the money, shakes her hips, and turns to the next customer. Down the bar, another girl in jean shorts frantically mops up spilled beer with a handful of dollar bills before jamming them into the register.

We're looking down at six shots of tequila and three bottles of beer. Jack and I convince Kevin to take one shot with us, then Jack and I take another shot, then Jack and Kevin each take a beer and I take the last shot of tequila. It's a decent start.

Now that I've got a slight buzz going I glance over and notice a cute little girl standing across the room. She's wearing a damp, white tank top and no bra. Her body is magnificent, but it's her face that really does it for me. There's a sweetness there, a pseudo-innocence... Just the combination to sucker the drunks in.

I mention the girl to Jack and begin planning how to approach her. He is less impressed than I, but appreciates the sentiment. She seems busy with some other people, though, so I turn and watch the girls working the bar. Then, when I turn back around the tank top girl is standing nearby, staring at me.

"SHE WANTS TO TALK TO YOU, DUDE!" Jack says grinning, then turns away to order more drinks.

"WHAT DID HE SAY TO YOU?" I inquire, smiling, playing it cool.

"HE SAID, 'I THINK YOU'RE PRETTY CUTE, BUT NOT NEARLY AS MUCH AS MY FRIEND DOES.' HE SAID YOU THINK I'M DOWNRIGHT BEAUTIFUL."

"HE SAID THAT?"

"YEAH."

"WELL, YEAH, PRETTY MUCH," I say, and try to grin devilishly.

We talk for a minute. Shout into each other's ears is what I really mean. Where are you from? What's your story?

The conversation pauses and she just stares at me for a while, like she is mystified by something.

"YOU HAVE THE MOST BEAUTIFUL FACE," she finally says.

"WHA-," I stutter, taken aback, "Thank you. Er-"

"WHAT?"

"THANK YOU. YOU HAVE A PRETTY BEAUTI-FUL FACE, TOO."

And we stare into each other's eyes, our faces just a few inches apart. I know I should kiss her, but I can't. I just can't find it inside me. Picking women up in bars isn't my thing when it comes right down to it. It turns me off.

Pretty soon she gets confused and wanders away. Says

maybe we'll chat more later, but I know we won't. She won't give me that chance to embarrass her again.

As the tank top girl walks away, I notice a sour-looking fellow staring hard at me. Like he is trying to be intimidating or something. I ignore him and go back to boozing with Jack and Kevin. Jack wonders what happened with the girl, but I blow it off. We have another drink.

"WHAT'S UP WITH THIS GUY?" Jack wonders, turning my attention back to the sour-faced guy. He has sidled his way up to our group and has his arm wrapped jovially around Kevin's neck.

It's that "alpha male" sort of physical intimidation thing that some guys start doing when they're drunk. That some assholes do all the time. Pseudo-friendly, half threatening. Jack thinks this guy had his eye on the girl in the tank top. He's trying to stir up trouble, but it's a mystery why he has focused his attentions on Kevin.

Jack grabs the guy's arm.

"YO MAN, WE'RE NOT GAY, DUDE."

"WHA-"

"YO! IT'S COOL, MAN, IT'S COOL, BUT WE'RE NOT GAY. JUST LETTING YOU KNOW."

"WHAT?!"

Jack turns around and chuckles, while the "Mr. Tough Guy" lets go of Kevin and turns to face us. I can see one of his friends looking over, watching everything intently, ready for a fight.

For some reason Tough Guy decides not to talk to Jack, but instead turns back to Kevin to respond.

"I'M JUST TALKING TO YOU GUYS. JUST TRYING TO BE FRIENDLY. I'M NOT GAY."

Now I'm starting to wonder if he really is gay.

"WHY DON'T YOU WANT TO BE FRIENDS

WITH ME?" Jack shouts with a hint of menace in his voice.

"WHAT?"

"WHY ARE YOU BOTHERING MY BOY HERE, WHY DON'T YOU WANT TO BE FRIENDS WITH ME?"

"I'M NOT TALKING TO YOU," Tough Guy says, turning back to Kevin.

"I'M TALKING TO YOU, MAN!" Jack says angrily.

This whole time Kevin just sits facing the bar, trying to ignore the situation, hoping it will go away.

"WHAT'S YOUR PROBLEM, MAN," Tough Guy says, turning to Jack.

"WHY YOU PUTTING YOUR HAND ON MY BOY? THAT'S NOT COOL, MAN. IF YOU WANT TO TALK TO SOMEBODY, WHY DON'T YOU TALK TO ME."

Tough Guy's confidence wavers. He mumbles something inaudible to Jack, then turns to me.

"THAT GIRL YOU WERE TALKING TO IS PRETTY CUTE, ISN'T SHE."

"YEAH, MAN, SHE'S A REAL CUTE GIRL," I say, staring him down.

"I'M PETE, GUYS, I DIDN'T MEAN ANY OFFENSE."

We each shake his hand politely, but when he gets to me he glares and tries to crush my hand in his grip. He's not nearly strong enough, though, so I just stare him down again and pretend it didn't happen. Finally, he turns and starts to walk away.

"I'M NOT YOUR KID BROTHER, ALRIGHT!" Kevin shouts suddenly into Pete's retreating back.

It's a perfect punctuation to the whole ridiculous

exchange. We order another round.

A large group of sailors enters the bar, and a drunk, blonde woman next to us is fascinated by them. She is wearing a pin-striped business suit and looks to be in her late 20s. Her professional bearing contrasts oddly with her advanced state of inebriation.

"OH MY GOD! I WANT TO WEAR HIS HAT!" she tells me, pointing at one of the sailors' hats. "HIS HAT IS, LIKE, SO COOL; I WANT TO WEAR IT. DO YOU THINK HE'LL LET ME WEAR HIS HAT??"

"SURE, JUST GO ASK HIM, I BET HE WILL," I tell her.

"OH MY GOD! DO YOU REALLY THINK HE'LL LET ME WEAR IT? I REALLY WANT TO WEAR IT."

After a few more, similar exchanges, she takes my advice and approaches the sailor. He puts his officers' hat on her head and begins kissing her passionately without uttering a single word. They go at it for a while.

"SAILOR GIRL!" Jack screams, laughing, "NICE HAT!"

She glances up at us like maybe she noticed what he said and maybe she didn't, then buries herself deeper in the sailor's embrace.

The crowd thins out a little bit and becomes more raucous. The barmaids all take turns dancing on the bar, and as they shake their hips, the huge, old, wooden platform rocks precariously back and forth. The beer taps flip forward and back, on and off, and Jack seizes the opportunity to top his drink off.

"HAHA, FREE BEER! I TOLD YOU, DUDE, I TOLD YOU!"

Kevin bails on us to go home and get some sleep. The "scene" is getting to be too much for him. We wish him well and order another round. Jack has his eye on one of the bar maids, but it doesn't look like they will be hooking up with any customers tonight, just teasing them.

The beer taps continue to flip back and forth, pouring gallons of libation down the drain. Eventually the drain itself fills up with napkins and garbage, and starts flooding onto the bar, sort of like a fountain. The crowd grows quieter, but crazier. The barmaids are working triple-time now to try and keep people drinking and rake in as much cash for the night as possible. I don't think they're giving out free drinks anymore.

"Don't go into the bathroom, dude," Jack tells me soberly as he reappears after wandering off for a while. "Everything is covered in puke and shit."

"What? That's where I'm going right now. I gotta take a leak."

"Oh, shit! Hahaha, don't slip, dude. Don't slip! Or use the women's bathroom, man. Yeah, do that, trust me."

I approach the crowded women's room warily, wondering how this will work. A girl bursts through the bathroom door and runs past me screaming,

"Oh my God, all the toilets in there are overflowing!"

Dirty water begins to seep out from under the door. Most of the girls waiting in line are oblivious, but a few take on ashen expressions as they quickly weigh their bathroom needs against their bathroom options. My bladder feels like it's going to explode already, so I hold my breath, hike up my pants, and plunge into the men's room.

The floor is covered with dirty toilet-water, shit, and puke. Both sinks are stopped up with paper towels and puke, one of them is running over. The urinals are all stopped up with paper towels, piss, and... puke. Two of them are overflowing with it. There seems to be someone using one of the stalls, but the other one is completely stopped up and filled with shit.

I tiptoe up to the least-full urinal and relieve myself, trying to keep from getting any shit from the floor onto my pants. Then I rush back out, being ever so careful not to slip and fall.

The barmaids are still dancing, the sailor girl is still wearing her sailor's hat (but hooking up with two different sailors now, while the hatless original fellow chats up some other girls), and Jack is standing at the bar watching the dancing barmaids, laughing.

"It was bad, wasn't it, man?" he says as I come back to the bar.

"Can you imagine, someone has to clean that shit up in the morning," I say.

"Someone has to clean that shit up every morning, dude. I'd quit my job. I'd just quit my job."

"No amount of money is worth that," I agree, "and the poor fucker who cleans it is probably making minimum wage."

"No amount of money, dude."

The bar itself has filled up like a basin, and starts to overflow. I jump back as beer cascades onto my lap.

"Oh shit!" one of the barmaids exclaims, and rushes over to close the taps.

"Woohoo!" Jack cheers, pumping his fist.

We step outside to get some fresh air and wind down the night. The sailor girl is outside too, but has lost her sailor hat. Over the course of the evening we've seen her hooking up with several different sailors, all while wearing the same original hat, but she has finally lost it and, instead of sailors, settled her attention on a large group of screaming frat boys. They all have ridiculous grins stamped across their faces and are trying enthusiastically to hail a cab.

"Ok, but where are we going?" Sailor Girl says as she kisses one of them.

They hail a minivan cab and start cramming into it. Four of them in the back of the group also hail a regular cab, as there are about ten frat boys total, along with Sailor Girl.

"Sailor Girl!" Jack and I call perversely from the sidewalk, prompting her to turn back around as she is climbing into the minivan.

"Sailor Girl!" we shout a second time, and execute our best attempt at a sailor's salute. She laughs, then looks confused, then almost throws up, then turns around and crawls into the back of the minivan.

"Yahoo-oo!" the frat boys cry as their two cabs speed off into the night.

"Damn, dude."

"Dayum!"

"Gang bang time, man," Jack says.

"There was, like, ten dudes there, man."

"Gang bang bang."

"Damn, man, just damn. That's crazy."

"Ten dudes, hahaha, Sailor GIRL! Haha."

"It's sad. How does a person even end up that fucked up."

"You know, she's just like any other girl, man," Jack muses philosophically, "Probably she had some bad first boyfriend that couldn't fuck; got confused and mixed up about things. Maybe her dad didn't love her or something, you know. And she ends up drunk in bars trying to patch up all her holes and not knowing how."

"Yeah, maybe."

"It's a crazy, fucked up world, man. Sailor Girl."

"It's a mad world, man."

Jack and I start walking home. It's 3:30 a.m. and our apartment building isn't far away. I'm trying to walk fast so I can get back to my apartment to take a piss. Jack is walking slower, savoring the opportunity for drunken, philosophical conversation.

"Man, maybe I should have taken that girl in the tank top home," I say. "She was really cute."

"Yeah, man."

"Said my face was beautiful. I was like, huh?"

"She's a dirty girl, dude."

"I guess so. Cute, though. Not as dirty as Sailor Girl."

"Nobody's as dirty as Sailor Girl."

"Heh."

"You ever take a girl like that home, be sure to double bag it, man."

"Ha!"

There's something about beer that it runs directly from my throat into my bladder with no stops along the way. That's why I don't normally drink beer. Worse for me than most people, I mean. I'm more of a tequila man. Mexican nectar. Blue agave.

The point is, I did drink some beer, and I really have to piss at this point. Like, *really*. And pissing in the street is truly not my style. Give me some bushes, trees, a hedgerow perhaps – no problem. Not out in the street.

But Jack really wants to have that drunken conversation thing. He lives for it. You know the conversation, where it seems really important, and emotional, and profound at the time, but in the morning you don't remember what you said. Where you probably tell your friends something you didn't mean to tell, some secret, or private foible, or bit of gossip about somebody else, and the next day you hope that they don't remember it, if you even know what it was, because you probably don't. You talk in long, rambling sentences... But the weird thing is that it *is* important. That shared moment of vulnerability among drunks; it bonds people together. It's the crazy glue that many social circles, and not a few families, depend on. So even though it's stupid, even when you know it is, you can't just say, "You're drunk. Fuck you. I'm going home." At least not if you want to keep your friends, because then you broke the code. Unless they are really, truly being an ass, and then it's ok. According to the code.

I don't mind the drunken conversation so much, most of the time. I'm pretty tolerant of it. Sometimes I even embrace it. The problem is when I need to piss. Like now. And the problem is when I want to drop into my bed and go to sleep after I piss. Like now. And not talk to any of my damn friends any more.

Maybe I shouldn't go here, I don't know, but since I'm drunk at this point in the story, I hope you will humor me and maybe in the morning you can pretend you don't remember what I said...

See, the thing that just occurred to me is, like, I have no idea what it feels like when a woman needs to piss. I mean, like, I can't even imagine it. 'Cause the thing is, for me, when I need to piss, the real brunt of the pain, I mean the real source, the real "ouch factor", is in... like, my "member". Ok? Just a bit behind the head. I mean, sure you get the tremors in your bladder, "pain", but the real immediate, real *painful* source of pain is, you know, up there, near the head of the thing. And ladies don't have one of those things, so... See what I'm saying? Just saying is all.

And that's the kind of pain I'm in now. *That* pain. Intense. Like, I've really got to find a bathroom and go to bed. But Jack is going on about women, and the past loves of his life. Like, if I was by myself, I would be *running* home right now. And I don't want to raise the point to Jack, because I don't want to get into the whole pissing conversation, which I like to mostly keep to myself and try not to bother anyone with. And he's going to try to convince me just to piss on the bumper of somebody's car or something, and then that will be a whole argument because we're both drunk. The whole thing is moving towards the point of no return where I'm either going to piss myself or else my bladder is going to explode, which *is* possible, by the way.

And *the pain*, man.

Now Jack is lighting up a cigarette and starting to talk about his parents.

"Sorry, man, I really have to piss."

Then I run.

CHAPTER 10

THE THIRD TIME that Adam rose before dawn to discover Eve asleep, shivering outside his door, marked a new phase in their relationship.

Wordlessly, he scooped her up and carried her inside. Eve's eyes fluttered open briefly, then remained shut, and she clung to him. Adam lay her gently on the bed, and covered her with his heavy coat. Kneeling, he breathed in the scent of her hair, and kissed the plaited knot of it on top of her head. Then he caught hold of her hand, which squeezed affectionately back against his own. He kissed her mouth. Eve kissed back, giggling, but refused to open her eyes, burrowing deep down into the bedding and pulling his jacket tightly around her.

Adam squeezed her hand a final time and tore himself away. He walked back outside to begin the day's labor. An hour later Eve joined him, rubbing the sleep out of her eyes with the cleansing, soapy rays of the rising sun. She chose one row over, and imitated his labor.

"You don't need to sleep outside, you know," Adam told her. "You are more than welcome to come into the tower any time you wish. I will always be glad to see you."

Eve yawned at him groggily.

"But so late? It doesn't seem right," she said.

"Well sleeping outside shivering against the wall doesn't seem right to me," Adam said. "I have a large warm bed, you are always welcome to half of it. It would only give me pleasure to feel you lying beside me, no matter what hour you arrive."

"That would be scandalous."

Eve looked away, as if this concluded the conversation.

"Then I will sleep on the floor, or you can. Just come inside next time. My home is your home."

Adam said these words without thinking, but so sincerely, unreservedly. Eve was touched. It turned things around inside of her – twisted her perspective. She knew it for manipulation, but it felt good.

"Thank you, Adam. Ok, next time I will come inside. Anyway, it's good to see you. Did you miss me?"

"Of course I missed you. Don't even say it. I always miss you when you're gone."

Not knowing how to respond to this declaration, Eve continued silently with the work. She went down the row inspecting the leaves of the plants, breaking off diseased ones and discarding them.

"I miss you, too, Adam," she said finally, softly, "when I'm gone."

"When will you leave today, how much time do we have together?" Adam asked soberly.

"I don't know."

"Why don't you stay and eat dinner with me again this evening. I've caught a large catfish and need help devouring it."

"That would be nice."

"Anyway, the real reason is because I want you to stay here longer," Adam corrected himself.

"I know," Eve rubbed an onyx bead against her neck unconsciously.

She glanced across the fields, now outlined distinctly against the wild backdrop of the forest. Symmetrical, organized, lush with flowering rooted creatures. Soon to bear fruit. She looked again at the laborer who worked so many hours, so assiduously, alone. Eve was growing to hate being alone. She had spent too much of her time that way. Adam was still new to it. Even as these thoughts brushed across her mind, Eve was tense.

"Adam, there's a reason I came so early to see you this morning. I found something in the woods. A track. I think it is a leopard."

He stared at her blankly, then his eyes grew wide.

"Wha–! Where?"

"About three miles from here, beside a stream."

"And you slept outside?!"

"I'm not afraid of anything in this forest," Eve said, a gentle shade of defiance in her voice.

"What do you mean by that?" Adam asked incredulously. "You think you are invincible? What if something happened to you?"

"I am the forest's queen, and everything in it is subject to me. Including you," Eve winked and grinned at him endearingly, enjoying his concern. "But I have never seen a leopard before. You have. Would you come with me today, to look at the tracks? If there is a leopard wandering near here, I need to know. And you need to know."

"Of course. Of course I will," Adam said hoarsely, overcome with worry. "When I was attacked by the leopard before, that was a few days' walk from here. I don't know why, I just, for some reason I didn't think that it would come this far out."

"Adam, there may be more than one."

"That's true, but," he stammered, "but – nobody in York had ever seen one before and–"

"Nor in Atlantis."

"Right, so they must be incredibly rare. Anyway, I can definitely recognize the tracks."

Eve stood next to him and ran her fingers across the raw, pink scars on his chest, wincing. Adam stared hypnotically at her hand.

"How large was it?" Eve asked, an empathetic tremor in her voice.

"It was large," Adam said, "longer than I am tall. Two, three times heavier than I am."

"My God."

"We should go check those tracks soon," he said worriedly, scanning the line of trees at the field's edge.

"I was thinking, if I help you we can get all your work done by midday. Then–"

"No, let's go now."

"Ok. When the sun gets a little higher we will go. Until then I will help with your work."

"You don't have to help me, Eve, I can spare the time."

"I know," she said simply, rooting a sproutling weed out of the ground and casting it aside.

An hour later, Eve led Adam through the woods in search of the mysterious tracks she had seen.

"You don't need to bring your shovel."

"I needed it last time," Adam said, without explanation.

Even as they walked, Eve introduced Adam to new secrets of the forest. Fruits and plants he had scarcely known existed. She showed him where to look for them, how to collect them. Adam watched her distractedly, perpetually amazed at how naturally Eve traversed the forest. How much she knew. And how beautiful she was, in so many ways. She spotted wild creatures even before he did, and moved through the bushy undergrowth, thorns, brambles, with speed and grace that was magical. Truly the forest's queen.

Eve showed Adam the wild herbs she had used to make the poultice for his chest, and how to combine them. Every track and wild trail was known to her, and she tested his own knowledge as they went, challengingly, affectionately – nearly as amazed by Adam as he was by her.

"The tracks were just up here," she whispered warily, as the trickling sound of a forest stream began to reach their ears.

Adam gasped when the tracks came into view, deeply imprinted in the wet earth. He knelt to look closely at them. Broad, round, padded bowls pressed into drying mud. Sets of pinprick impressions betrayed their retracted claws.

"So it is a leopard," Eve commented, watching him.

"At least, the tracks look the same," Adam said, unwilling to vocalize the beast's existence.

Eve walked along the tracks' length, imagining a leopard stalking past.

"The gait is odd, though," she said. "See here? It's sort of lopsided."

"Probably the same leopard that attacked me," Adam said, "I injured one of its legs."

"Should we try to find it?"

"I don't know. We're probably not a match for him. We're probably better off just to avoid it. Do you have to go to this part of the woods?"

"I don't have to."

"Well, don't then. I won't either. Just be extra careful now that you know about it, and try to stay in places where he's not."

"It's scary, Adam."

Adam stared into space. Imagined Eve wandering through the forest alone. Often for days at a time. Sleeping in trees. Could leopards climb?

"Maybe tomorrow I will go looking for it," he said. "These tracks are a few days old, it could be anywhere."

"I haven't seen any other signs," Eve said. "Don't even think about doing it without me. I'm a better tracker than you are, and I know more about the forest."

"I won't put you in danger, Eve."

"Don't be ridiculous."

The words felt cold and Eve regretted them.

"I must return to Atlantis tomorrow," she said. "Wait until I return, then we can decide what to do together."

Adam was silent.

"Adam, don't make me bandage you up again, I won't be able to bear it. We've seen what we can here, let's go back to New York now."

"Will you sleep in the tower tonight, at least? With me and safe from the leopard?"

"Will you promise not to go looking for it until I get back?"

Adam paused for a long time.

"Ok, I promise."

"Ok."

Eve stood close to him, looking into his eyes. She touched between his eyebrows with the tip of her finger. They kissed passionately.

"I would have stayed with you anyway, but this is even better," she said, and her eyes flashed brightly in the merry, ephemerally carefree way that they did.

saxophone solo w/ drums introduction

                    This isn't related, per se, but it goes here. I don't know where else to fit it in. Maybe because of the violence to come.

You're probably wondering what the point of mixing all these stories together is. And what they have to do with Adam and Eve and New York. Or what New York has to do with Adam and Eve.   Or something like that. I've wondered the same thing many times.

Like, I don't know. That's just the way it seemed to fit together. Hold on until the end and see what you think. Things hang together that way sometimes. Maybe you see what I mean.

Evil runs to money,
Today I met a piece of shit.
Or money to evil?

How people he corrupted?
Yet it's so transparent.
How beautiful things wasted?

Or,
Money is weak.
Evil becomes its strength.

SATURDAY NIGHT IN the wintertime, a pretty lazy day. Maybe I did some laundry or something. I'm sure I was lonely. At 7 p.m., I called Jack to see what was going on.

"Dude," he said, "my friend Lee is in town, it's so cool! We're just hanging out up here with Paulie. Have you met Lee? No? Dude, come up and have a drink with us!"

I walked upstairs to Jack's apartment, happy to have company. After hollering and introductions, they poured me a drink. I'd hung out with Paulie a few times before, but Lee, a friend of theirs from college, was a new face to me. I sat easy and enjoyed my alcohol while the three of them caught up with each other. There was music in the background, Jack always had music going. I was drinking tequila. After a little while, conversation turned to what we should do for the evening.

Toe-tapping and discussion of the 'umm... um... we could...' variety ensued. There was no plan. There never is, really, that's half the point. I was indifferent, being mostly along for the ride. My evening's priority was to meet cute girls, which would be inevitable on a Saturday night out in the Village.

We stepped into the cold and walked to a little bar a few blocks away. It was your average sort of 'Irish Pub' in Manhattan: Guinness on tap, some plain wooden tables, an old wood bar to sit at. Sometimes there is even a dusty framed article on the wall describing the provenance of the wooden counter in question. Lee called a business friend to meet up with us. The bar was loud and mostly full.

We squeezed into a place in the back and scanned the scene. I noticed an absence of cute girls, but didn't say anything about it. The night was young. A waitress near us spilled a full tray of Jägermeister shots onto a man's back. In a miraculous feat of dexterity, she caught every single shot glass on the tray again as they bounced off of his back and tumbled towards the floor. The man had a stiff lip, bleached hair that was parted down the middle, and was wearing a luxurious white sweater. His head and face might have come from the set of a Gatsby film. The sweater was straight out of Aspen. I should say that the sweater had been white, because now it was purple and white. With his back drenched, he nevertheless tried to pretend that nothing had happened in order to not interrupt the conversation he was having with the woman next to him. The waitress grabbed two handfuls of napkins, though, and began frantically wiping at his back and apologizing. For a few seconds he froze, appearing not to know what to do. Then he tried to push her away in protest. No one in his party seemed to have any sympathy for him. We watched them and laughed a lot, and most of us drank a beer.

Jack and I, in particular, watched the Gatsby guy's group with a sociological interest. They were thirty-somethings who all knew each other, but didn't seem to like each other very much. They all seemed unhappy, like a true life version of that tv show, 'Friends'. We tried to imagine what they each did for a living, what their lives were like. More men streamed in, and women trickled out. Lee's business friend arrived. The unhappy thirty-somethings left, and we decided to leave too. Outside, we walked east through the Village and Jack described the expected trajectory of the evening to me.

"Look, bro, this is how it's gonna go down. Lee's goal for the evening is to go to one of these Korean head shops – some fuckin' place to get his dick sucked for $20, I don't know what else to call it – to go get his dick sucked by some hooker at a Korean massage parlor. Now in the meantime we're gonna go hit up another little club or two and just have a good time. I ain't going to no massage par- lor, I'll tell you that right now, you know, so at that point I'm gonna bounce. Now the thing is, Paulie's waiting for a callback from his cousin Fredrik who's uptown somewhere having a w-i-l-d party. I'm talking some sick shit, dude. So we may hear from him, we may not, but at any point in time, if Freddy calls and says come uptown, the shit's gonna go down, man, it's gonna hit the fan. We'll be up in some sick apartment overlooking Manhattan, drinking Cristal, with beautiful girls around us tearing their clothes off and shit. I am not fucking with you, man, it will be some unreal shit. Look, you're my boy, you can do whatever you want, you can get your dick sucked if you want. But don't get your dick sucked, dude, seriously. Haha, I'm fuck- ing with you, but I'm serious. I just want you to be, like, on the down low so you know what's up."

...Aight.

We walked to the Alphabet Lounge, which is a little bar

and music club in Alphabet City, the easternmost part of Greenwich Village. As you move east in Manhattan the avenues count down, for example from 5th Avenue to 4th Avenue, and so on to 1st Avenue, and then Avenue A, Avenue B, and Avenue C, hence the name of the neighborhood. Saturday was '80s Night at the Alphabet Lounge, so they would be playing classic dance hits from the 1980s. Take on me.

On the weekend it was a little skeptical whether our group of five men could even get into the Alphabet Lounge. A lot of clubs and lounges like that won't let you in if you don't have enough women with you. To most city people this detail is obvious, but I didn't know about it until I moved to New York. As it happened, the door was easygoing and waved us through. The place was packed – wall to wall people dancing, drinking, sitting and talking, laughing and yelling. The usual. We squeezed our way to the bar and ordered some drinks. A round of shots set the mood.

There's something about '80s music, especially '80s dance music. It's contagious. Something sort of naive and uninhibited. An impossibly superficial take on the world, one that could never last. But a knowing superficiality, not an ignorant one. It is music suited to a particular kind of happy grown-up party. Where you can sniff coke, or not, or wear a sport coat or not, or dance if you want to – or not. And it's ok. Something that seems to say, "Everything is good and happy and exciting and sexy, and it's not really but it is because we refuse to accept anything else!" That faux-naive infectiousness is an emotional seduction. Preachers even use it. Take on me, indeed.

We hadn't been there long when a group of Brazilian models descended on the Alphabet Lounge. I'll call them models, it's as good a guess as any. They were all young and tall and thin and beautiful, they were all Brazilian, and, it turned out, had all recently moved to New York. After a little while, the star of their group started giving me the come-on to dance with her. I'd been watching her and her female friends dirty dancing with each other and they seemed a bit overly affectionate, so I had some misgivings in my mind. She looked like fun to dance with, though, and I didn't hold back. Soon I was the envy of the club, dancing the night away with this tall, beautiful blonde. Jack met his own match in one of the Brazilian brunettes and quickly decided that he wanted to marry her.

"She's perfect, man," he told me during a lull. "She's my perfect, ideal woman. I want her to have my babies. Really, I want her to have my babies."

It's wonderful to dance with an unusually beautiful, tall, blonde woman. Maybe that is only a crystallization of cultural stereotypes, but it feels magnificent. I mean, dancing with unusually beautiful women is special, just in general, but if the unusually beautiful woman happens to be tall and blonde it is even more. As far as I could tell (the club was so packed that I couldn't get a good line of sight on her shoes), my lovely dancing partner was about the same height as me, or maybe slightly taller. She was curvy-willowy in the sexiest way, with soft copper skin and a delicately chiseled face.

Although I'm not intimidated by tall women at all, I do always sort of feel that when I'm with a woman who is equal to my height or taller she is just waiting around for a taller guy than me to come along. Whether that's mostly in my head or it's simple biological reality, I don't know. Some women actually prefer shorter men, but isn't that similar to men who prefer fat women? Do you want to be desired for your inadequacy? If I was dating a tall woman and I thought that one of the things she liked about me was that I was shorter than her it would be a major turn off. I would want her to wish I was taller, but love the other parts of me so much that she forgets it. If I smell bad, I want a woman who loves me even though I smell bad, not a woman who loves me because I smell bad! Like, what hell is wrong with people? But, anyway, I was dancing with the most beautiful girl in a crowded little dance club filled with beautiful girls, and it was good.

During another lull in the music, Jack came and pulled me aside.

"Hey man, you got my back, right?"

Words that bode well.

"What? Yeah. What's going on?"

He was pretty worked up.

"I went to get a drink and this guy moved in on the girl I was dancing with."

"Oh."

"I can't just let that girl walk away from me, man. I'm going to break that shit up."   Uh, what?

"Sure man," I said, "don't worry about it. I got you."

The blonde was pulling me back to dance some more, and I didn't want to disappoint her. As we started dancing again, I maneuvered myself next to Jack's brunette interest and her new partner. My adrenaline was flowing at a decent rate and I had to keep my eyes up so I could step in at any time if trouble started, but I tried to play it cool with the blonde girl at the same time. Probably nothing would happen, and being inconspicuous in that situation is the best thing – there's no reason to get someone's tension up and force them into a corner.

Jack made his move, squeezing in next to the brunette, grabbing her hands, and pulling her away. It was a pretty wild move. Her other dancing partner stood there confused, trying to understand what was happening. Then he got really annoyed and tried to squeeze back in between them, but Jack blocked him off. Then this resigned expression passed across his face and he backed up a bit and chatted with some of his friends – others in the Brazilian party. The brunette went along with it, but you could see she was uncomfortable, and she pulled away from Jack to get a drink after that song. He sat down at a booth our friends had secured. The other guy came over and had a word with him. Neither of them got angry, so I turned all my attention back to my own dancing beauty and we danced another song. After the song, she excused herself to go get a drink too. She wanted to talk to the brunette.

I found Jack still sitting at our booth, looking badly deflated. The story wasn't especially surprising – to me. I had already suspected the situation we were in. The fellow Jack had cut in on was a childhood friend of the brunette girl. He had told Jack, "I know you really like this girl and want to dance with her, and that's ok, but I think you should know that she's a lesbian." Jack had confirmed these things by running over and asking the brunette herself about it, before she had a chance to talk to his rival. Whatever the exact words exchanged were, they were enough to leave him convinced.

"It's so sad, man," he said. "That girl is perfect. What a waste."

I had assumed some of them were lesbians from the way they were dancing with each other, but I guess Jack hadn't seen that. Or didn't want to see it. Maybe that particular girl wasn't even a lesbian, maybe it was a convenient lie, and it was easier for Jack to believe it than to accept blunt rejection through disbelief. He accepted the story as truth easily, when he was normally a skeptical person. "But what is truth?" as John had Pilate say. Even when you know someone is straight or gay you don't really know. Maybe they don't know, either, really. We all see the world and the people around us and think we know so much, and often we barely even know ourselves. People change and who they are is not who they were, but they would have said they aren't that way. And they change again, and sometimes again. Or they don't. Often they never change, but still don't know who they are. Isn't the important part that they don't want you? It's not who they are, which you can probably never really know.

I didn't have much hope for myself and the blonde girl, anyway, but then she started ignoring me and I felt annoyed. A new group of men had come into the place, apparently specifically to meet these Brazilian girls there, and she was wasting her time talking to one of them instead of me. He was an ugly bastard, but at least 6'6" tall. I motioned for her to come dance with me again, but she turned away.

Well, she kept looking over at me though, even while talking to him, but I hardly credited it at the time. I reeled in what I considered to be my wounded pride and resolved to ignore her for the rest of the night. It wasn't hard to do, because all of a sudden –

"Oh, shit, Freddy's here!" Jack said, and his face broke into a grin.

Fredrik, dressed ridiculously, walked in like he owned the place and was planning to take a shit in the room. Mid-height and skinny, with a short goatee, he looked almost exactly like Kid Rock. He was wearing a sort of turban thing on his head and sported flowy, maroon, velvet pants with red-striped, Adidas high-top sneakers. I can't even really describe the shirts and jackets he was wearing, because there were a lot of them and they were weird.

"This place sucks," he concluded immediately. "Come on, let's go."

A slick looking Japanese man named Yosh followed Freddy everywhere and kept apologizing for him. Freddy was a bit, *snort*snort*, Yosh said, "but don't mind it."

Paulie grabbed my arm as our group headed for the door.

"Killer, don't you want to say goodbye to that beautiful blonde you were dancing with?"

"No man, fuck her. Let's go."

Without looking back I walked out the door, harmed by pride. And more than pride. I would have enjoyed so much to see that beautiful woman again. But what if I went back, and got her phone number, and we met up again. In that unlikely event. It would have been, at best, a cheap relationship. Wouldn't it? I wanted so much more, deeply. I wanted life to be so perfect and unmuddled. Wanted, not as conscious thought, but ingrained in my consciousness, so that I acted on it as if by instinct, without doubt or hesitation. In later weeks, Jack and I returned to the Alphabet Lounge several times, but never again saw such beautiful women there. The music was always good.

Outside, I tried to introduce myself to Freddy. I made an easygoing joke about how he was "all pimped out," but he took an immediate dislike to me. Or maybe that was why. I guess it was a mutual reaction, I hated him almost instantly, but I tried to give him the benefit of the doubt and be friendly. For the rest of the evening, he refused to talk to me or even make eye contact.

Jack would later tell me his stories about Freddy.

"The first time I met Freddy, man, I was going out with

his sister and we were at this big party that her family was throwing. Freddy grabs me around the neck and sticks his tongue in my ear. In my ear, man. Then he says, 'Now that you're going out with my sister, that's a present from my family to you.' I mean, how do you respond to that? It was some crazy shit."

Freddy's immediate and extended family included a Scandinavian prince, a handful of powerful industrialists, and a few of the 20th Century's most iconic movie stars. I knew this wasn't bullshit, because one of the movie stars was verifiably Paulie's grandmother. Paulie was born into the side of the family with relatively less money (and had a proportionately smaller coke habit). With the wealth and connections he was born into, Freddy could easily have settled into the life of jet setting around the world, coke sniffing, whoring and whatever. Debauchery. Most of his family supposedly did just that. And it was more than evident that Freddy did, too. But for Freddy, it was not enough – he wanted more from life, so he became an international 'erotic filmmaker'. Within ten minutes of our meeting him in the East Village he was telling us about a new private website where for $10,000 you could get almost any porn star in the world to fly almost anywhere in the world and have sex with you.

"Only $10,000, man. Anywhere in the world!" he said enthusiastically, encouraging us to try it, with the manner of describing a favorite pizza joint.

We objected a little to his disparagement of the Alphabet Lounge, but Freddy was insistent.

"No, no, no. Look there's a good place right there, right across the street."

Across the street, in which direction Freddy marched as he said the words, was Zum Schneider's, which is normally a nice little German brew-pub with tables and a bar and such. But tonight, keeping its character, things were a little bit different.

Tonight, the windows had been blocked out with black paper. Men and women of all ages were moving in and out of Zum Schneider's dressed in 18th Century fetish garb. Essentially, the women were dressed up as 18th Century whores and the men were dressed up as 18th Century — townsfolk? Sort of like pilgrims. We walked through the door and stumbled into a crazy swirl of lights, costumes, dancing, and semi-deviant behavior. Young girls and old men danced together in imitative mockery of an ancient waltz; transvestites and men in Amadeus-style wigs sat alone petulantly or chatted together; a few scattered normals looked confused; various kinds of smoke coagulated the air. The atmosphere was weird, perverse, and jovial. But self-consciously so.

It felt stranger than it was. Maybe that self-consciousness is why — there was nothing holding it together. The costumed assembly seemed to have arrived in couples and small groups that didn't mix. There was no apparent community, no noticeable connection between the employees and the crowd, no — congeniality. But they were trying hard at something. All these people. Hanging, rotating, twisting in place in a bizarre, stilted melee.

Alcohol was proceeded naturally through my body and I went to find the bathroom. The facilities were a trough covering two walls of a small room, with sparkly fish tank rocks in the bottom of it for character. German style pissing? I hoped that Fredrik wouldn't come hang his dick next to me. Jack was in there as well. I only remember the end of what he said.

"Stick close to me, man, this is going to be some crazy

shit tonight."

His protective attitude annoyed me, but I blew it off.

The rest of the night was anti-climactic, anyway. We stood around inside Zum Schneider's for about ten minutes and then left. Freddy called his limousine to pick us up and we all stood on the sidewalk trying to vibe. The limousine ran late and Freddy was irritated. It was already awkward without that.

Freddy was so obviously an asshole – ignoring, shouting over, sneering at, and occasionally insulting people directly – and all of us just sort of pretended to ignore it. Yosh continued apologizing for him and saying how Freddy didn't normally act that way, but the apologies grew quieter and more abbreviated, until he would only mouth the word 'sorry' sheepishly and look away. Yosh seemed alright, though; at least, he was friendly enough and nice to everyone. I read him as someone very privileged, but maybe the opposite was the case. Jack told me that the first time they met, Yosh was dressed up in women's lingerie, twirling around a pole in some funked out night club. Jack had ended up there in pretty much the same way I had ended up in Zum Schneider's tonight. That must have been "some crazy shit," too.

We stood bunched on the sidewalk in the wind and cold. Freddy continued to be loud, insensitive, and deprecating. Lee fantasized out loud about Korean whores. Paulie repeatedly challenged Yosh to a 'fight', and repeatedly lost. Lee's business friend laughed nervously and didn't know what to say. Jack tried to be social glue and hold everyone together. I tried to stay relaxed and just be nice. I don't know how to feel about that.

A fine line distinguishes being easy and non-judgmental from being enabling and complicit. In times like that I don't know where I fell. We don't want to alienate our friends in their moments of weakness, or call attention to others' flaws when we are so painfully aware of our own.

Perhaps I am unfair to him, but it felt like Fredrik was really evil. He was wrong in a way that made your skin literally crawl. This person in front of you was bad inside, in the fat below their surface flesh were squirming cockroaches. He felt like my natural enemy, he and I both seemed to feel that. But it didn't feel good. Maybe satisfying.

How does it feel to be beholden to another's money? Jack wasn't. I wasn't. I never was. The rest were. Was I? They were pathetic. For me it would feel suicidal. If you sink so low in your heart you may as well kill yourself. You're already dead inside. Is that too harsh? I believed things like that.

Jack and I decided to walk home. I wished everyone the best and tried to give Fredrik a polite, "take it easy, man." Nicety gets the best of me. He turned away and didn't acknowledge it. Jack and I wandered back through the Village. We talked about the night, about the Gatsby guy and his friends, about the Brazilian lesbians, and Freddy and Yosh, and money and women. Jack told me stories about him and Paulie and Lee. And we sort of propped each other up, psychologically, so that the next day each of us could get up again and stand before the beautiful fucked world. Jack was idealistic enough. Not as much as I, but enough.

I walked into my apartment alone, lay on my bed in my clothes, and didn't bother to close my eyes against the ceiling's hard, fluorescent light. It had been a strange night, a night like a dream. For some people here every night is like that one. Every night is a dream, even for the best of us.

People get caught in strange ones, for strange reasons, or even mundane. Most of us choose our dreams, whether we want to admit it or not. And the bigger the dream the more it was chosen. We chose the broad themes and life painted in the details and colors. Sometimes it came out askew.

CHAPTER 11

THAT NIGHT EVE DID sleep in Adam's bed. Innocent, they slept almost like two children together. Although some things came naturally. Adam and Eve awoke the next morning in each other's arms. Quietly happy, a little bit confused.

Eve left for Atlantis the next morning. Adam wanted to go with her, or at a minimum to see her safely through the woods. Eve rejected the idea completely. This was not the first time the subject had come up, but it meant more now.

"I don't advise you go looking for Atlantis!" Eve had warned him once. "People don't often complete the journey on their own. Alive, if you know what I mean."

She was gentler now, but as firm in her resolve. She bade him farewell abruptly, and disappeared into the woods more quickly than he could follow. Allowing little argument. She promised to return within the week.

It was not from warning or trepidation that Adam failed to search out Atlantis on his own. Even with the leopard in the woods, he had little fear. Nor even the work on his garden at New York. He had long ago caught up the lost initial pace, and spent the better part of many days improving his tower home, fishing, or exploring the ancient ruins. Adam was fascinated by Atlantis, of course. More so than he could easily express. Not only was it the mysterious home of the woman he loved, it was the only real city other than York that he had ever heard of, or begun to imagine. The only place he could have gone to see new people, to discover unknown things. The idea of it turned his mind nearly inside out. A new city, a new people – Atlantis! Legends and faerie tales.

There was only one thing Adam desired more deeply. To make Eve happy. To see the smile on her face again when she saw him. The glowing love within her eyes, beaming out into his own and charging them. It seemed so important to Eve that he not follow her; she seemed to depend on it. Almost desperately, when he pressed the point. Adam would never betray her trust.

So instead of that, he did the next best thing to ease his mind. He went looking for the leopard.

This seemed fair.

If Eve would run away so quickly, through the dangerous woods by herself, then he would hunt the leopard while she was gone. He would never have allowed Eve to join him in the hunt, anyway. Too dangerous. Somehow, Adam believed, Eve understood this silent compromise. She knew that he would seek out the leopard, even if it terrified her, even if she hoped he wouldn't.

Adam secured his long glass knife to his belt, took the sharp stone shovel in hand, and went in search of the monster that had almost killed him.

He returned to the tracks and followed their path as far as he could trace it, then branched out into the forest, trying to imagine where a leopard might stalk its prey, or make its home. Mostly, he searched along the river bank and around the larger streams and ponds nearby. The forest sparkled with subtle noise and movement of uncounted life. Adam searched for the dead space — the silent, washing, waked tunnel of stillness that would follow a terrifying predator through these woods.

A blue jay whistled at him, amused by Adam's serious demeanor. Vultures called overhead, loudly, announcing death, and the soon to be new life in their blood. Several of them, in a frenzy, sounding out their presence with unmistakable pride. Adam could not see through the thick canopy to locate them precisely. Not even from a clearing.

The day wore on, and he was forced to return to his tower garden fruitless. The following day he searched again, starting at daybreak, seeking the carcass that the vultures had found. He did not find it, and he did not find the leopard.

Perhaps it had left that part of the forest. Adam hoped so. He was not sure where else to search, he had seen no other signs. And the garden was beginning to resent his neglect. Against his will, he knew he should devote another day to cultivating. It would give him a chance to rethink his hunting strategy.

Adam's work the next day in the garden was fitful and conflicted. His only thought of a leopard wandering the woods in which Eve worked. A beast likely to attack a man, not to mention a young woman. As much as Adam respected Eve's abilities, her hardiness and harmony with the natural world, it was not enough. Not nearly enough. He couldn't sleep.

At dawn he resumed his search through the forest. Quickly now, feverishly, relinquishing all regard for his own welfare in favor of a confrontation. He did not find it. But late that afternoon, in the thick heart of the forest, he discovered the scent of rotting flesh. The bushy, covered ground betrayed no tracks, but, guided by the heavy odor alone, Adam found its source.

His stomach turned over.

An oily skull grinned up at him. A large stag. It's mostly eaten corpse was torn and broken, half strewn across the ground. Two, three days old. Looking closely, Adam made out the faint, telltale impressions that vulture beaks had left on the bones. Here and there, more disturbingly, were deep gouged tooth marks. Ground into the skull. Adam picked up a thick, eviscerated section of ribs. The bones were snapped, pulverized.

The next morning Adam searched again, but found nothing. He returned to New York at midday, frustrated, trying to imagine how to build a trap for the leopard.

Eve sat alone in the middle of the garden, singing. Adam heard her before he could see her.

"One thousand archers stand upon brave Atlantean wall.
One thousand archers and a man.
One dear to me.

Sing beautifully through the night
With burning arrow's bows.
One thousand men on brave Atlantean wall.
One dear to me.
My one life light.

Come morning you will free us from our plight.

Where have you gone, brave archers,
Who stood upon our wall?
Where have your feet been thrown to,
Where wounded, where did fall?

The war at last is over,
For forever and a day,
Poor thousand spirits left to guard us.
Poor dear, beloved ghost
To guide my way."

His heart raced at the sound of her voice. A smile spread irresistibly across his lips. Eve had never come back so quickly before. He had doubted she would keep her word to return within the week, she had rarely held to such promises in the past. Breaking into a run, Adam rushed to shed the forest, to catch broad sight of his love and greet her. Such a little human thing that meant so much.

Eve sat cross legged in the middle of Adam's garden, already lush with green. Perhaps it was her garden too, she worked on it enough. She was arranging wildflowers into a bouquet, her brow knitted in concentration.

Adam stood at the edge of the field and watched her, enjoying the chance to catch Eve unawares. He slid the long knife out of his belt and dropped it quietly to the ground, hoping to allay any suspicions she might raise about his activities in the forest. Far off, at the other edge, something moved through the tall grass around the field, but was lost upon the occupied horizons of Adam's mind.

"Eve!" he called, and waved.

She stood up beaming, with her arms folded across her chest. Tan and orange and black slinked across the field. Subtly. Slowly accelerating. Adam broke into a run.

"Where have you been? I've been waiting all day," Eve called out impetuously.

"Eve!"

Living terror played across Adam's face.

"Eve! Run!"

"What?" she stared in confusion as Adam charged towards her, his shovel held high, threatening.

The leopard's roar broke across the air, shaking them. Eve screamed in surprise and spun about, then sunk to her knees in shock. It seemed on top of her already. She brought her arms up across her face.

Red tunneled haze overcame Adam's vision. Time slowed. It seemed to stop. He moved forward as if he were not moving at all. The shovel floated out of his hands, he gained speed, yet his legs barely seemed to stretch across the ground. Eve's knees slid through empty air and printed into the earth. Her face faded to white, then her arms slowly, excruciatingly, concealed it from his view. The leopard sunk into the ground to spring.

Adam flew past her. Like lightning from out of the clear sky, he arced blindingly, irresistibly into the leopard's path. Never slowing, predestined to be grounded and explode.

The monster snarled, and wheeled angrily. Violently clenching up the muscles in his legs, nearly snapping the tendons, Adam ground to a halt in front of it, positioning himself between the leopard and Eve. Subtly, proudly, it inched backwards away from him. Adam raised his hands above his head and shouted angrily. The leopard growled a low, slow, rumbling warning and they watched each other, trapped together in time.

Then it pounced. The leopard's heavy body somehow sliced the air, and was on top of him.

"No!" Eve's cry filled the still space between the city walls and tall forest trees.

Sorely wounded, Adam caught the beast tightly in a wrestling grip, swinging onto its back and locking his arms around its neck. Blood washed his body. The leopard turned dark from the stream.

It roared chokingly, and thrashed, boiling the air with its long claws. Adam wrapped his legs around its chest like a constrictor, tightening farther down each time the monster tried to breathe, gradually squeezing the air out of its lungs.

His arms compressed more closely around its neck.

The leopard rolled and pitched across the ground. It tried to stand and run, but gasping need for oxygen brought it tremoring back to earth, where it lay still a moment, then thrashed again, locked tight in Adam's unrelenting grip.

Eve circled the tumbling bodies, hysterical. She drew a small knife from out of her belt, and wondered what to do with it. Then, watching for a quiet moment, she plunged the knife into one of the leopard's eyes. It squealed pitifully. The two locked bodies twisted violently across the ground and knocked Eve over. She leapt up to resume her assault, but churning paws warded her off. She could find no way around them.

Where it could be seen, where the coursing blood rubbed off against the ground, or against the leopard's body, Adam's skin was white. Corpse like. His muscles trembled from exhaustion, but his grip on the leopard grew ever tighter. Spurred on by single minded, suicidal will, and deep, flushed wells of adrenaline.

Ages, eons later – a felt eternity – the leopard's body relaxed and ceased to move. Eve stabbed at it for good measure, but the monster was dead. Adam remained wrapped tautly around the corpse. His lips quivered disturbingly, his face a ghostly pallor. Only the whites of his eyes still gazed upon the horrific scene.

"Adam? Adam!"

Eve's voice could not reach him.

"Adam, it's over. It's dead," she said softly, plugging up a bleeding wound with one hand, and caressing his face with the other.

Adam did not respond. Lost in another world, a private hell. Cast in interminable battle with the leopard. His grip tightened still more firmly around its neck. Eve became frantic. She slapped him and screamed into his ears, but there was no response. Only the vision of a broken young man, white lips quivering morbidly in gray, cloudy light. Trapped in deadly embrace.

Eve could not allow it. She pried his fingers open one by one, trying not to break them. Lacking the strength to move his arms. One finger at a time, so slowly, as quickly as she could. The instant his grip was broken, Adam's entire body went slack and slumped to the ground. Eve gripped him under the shoulders and dragged him, one awkward step at a time, into the tower.

She went to work. Cleaning out his wounds with fresh water; staunching; bandaging; bringing up the fire and cauterizing with her steel knife. It was hard to say whether Adam's unconsciousness made the job more or less painful. Eve felt sure she must lose him. He had lost so much blood. She worked frantically, but efficiently, doing everything she could think of to repair his damaged body. Immediately, she began fashioning a whole stockpile of poultices and applied them as quickly as she could to the wounds where bleeding had been firmly stopped.

Eve worked late into the night, and finally collapsed beside Adam herself when she could think of nothing else to do. He had never made a movement, scarcely a moan, but he breathed. She lay beside him, resting her poor, tired head against his shoulder, sometimes kissing it and brushing it with tears. Catching fitful sleep.

Eve had never stayed with Adam in New York for more than a single night. This time she stayed three weeks, slowly nursing him back to life. The first seven days he barely moved. She came so close to losing him.

During the days when Adam lay unconscious in bed, or later, when he still hadn't the energy to get up, Eve tended his garden as best she could, keeping it healthy and strong. She couldn't do the job that Adam could, of course. Perhaps nobody could. Yet, she had some experience tending to plants, herself. Eve imitated what she had seen of Adam's methods, and supplemented them with her own ideas, filling in admirably. All while nursing Adam miraculously back to life.

For three days after the leopard's attack Adam lay senseless in his bed. Scarce breathing at times, at others moaning, or shivering and dripping with sweat. Eve trickled spoonfuls of broth into his mouth. He would burn with fever for half the day, then turn terribly, clammy cold.

On the fourth day, Adam blinked open his eyes. He raised his head, ever so slowly, and glanced about himself. The exertion caused not a little pain, and his head dropped back onto its pillow, but his eyes remained fixed on Eve.

"Adam? Can you hear me?" Eve asked breathlessly.

"I suppose this is heaven," he whispered.

"You're not yet so lucky as that," she said, sitting quickly beside him and replacing the wet rag across his forehead. "You wouldn't get away from me so easily, you know. You've just been sleeping for a few days, recovering your energy. You've given me quite a scare!"

He had already slipped back to sleep.

That night Adam awoke again, just for a moment. Eve woke too, instinctively, as soon as he opened his eyes. He felt her beside him in the dark. She lay her hand down gently on his chest, where it had not been wounded. Rubbed his skin ever so softly. Adam tried to pull her tight against him, but lacked the energy to move. She squeezed up closer, reading his mind.

Atlantean royal family, who had been a regular customer of her forest delicacies. As one of the younger Royal sons, the prince was given less wealth, but more freedom; he could marry whom he chose. By all accounts he was a good man. He claimed to have fallen in love with her. Eve scarcely knew him, but it was more than she had hoped for. She was excited to become a princess, even if a lesser one.

Yet, she spent every possible minute with Adam, returning to Atlantis only fitfully, when she absolutely must. The prince didn't seem to mind, neither did Adam. He did mind the prince.

"When the crop comes, I will return to York," Adam says pensively. "Why don't you come with me."

"Come with you?"

"Why don't you marry me. Would you?"

Eve stands still, looking at him. Awkwardly silent.

"Don't you even consider it?"

"Of course I consider it! Adam - but, I don't know."

A stillness passes between them. The lovers embrace, and cry together, quietly, not unhappily, but in pain.

"What do you want, Eve?"

"I don't know. I don't know what to want."

"Do—," he starts to speak, then changes to a whisper, "do you want me to tell you what to want?"

She glances about distractedly.

"I - no. No, don't."

Tears begin to dwell in Eve's eyes. She tries to imagine returning with Adam to York, but can't. As much as she loves him, as much as she would love to. She can scarcely believe in York's existence, it is like a dream that has gone one step too far. Though she really does believe, it doesn't seem real. Is it even a choice? Is it as much a choice as sprouting wings and flying to the moon? Touching the sun. And even if it is, what would she give up? So much. Everything? Or nothing at all, or her heart — or love? Tortured, Eve's mind closes down. Her heart begins to wall itself off.

"I just don't know. I don't know what I want. I want things to stay the way they are now. I don't want anything to change."

She squeezes him tightly in a moment's pause. Then something happens. She pulls away. The wall comes up behind her eyes, protecting her from him.

"Adam, I want to go back home and marry my husband, and live a normal life."

What was said after that did not matter. For all of what they felt, it did not matter. It hurt them.

Eve said she would come back again, but never did. She cried as she walked through the forest. Adam felt the touch of death inside him. Threw himself frantically into his work, exhausting memory, starving his brain's ability to think. He harvested an extraordinary crop, among the greatest York had ever seen, and carted it back to his home. Along the way he collected rare roots and medicinal herbs that Eve had shown to him. Tenderly, like they were a part of her. Bringing them back.

Word spread quickly as Adam marched up the long, stone path before the city walls. York's citizens stood upon the ramparts and cheered. Children rushed outside in throngs to greet him. His mother cried tears of joy and pride as he advanced from the distance. They barely noticed his scars.

Adam smiled warmly at everyone, casting off the melancholy underneath. He was back among the people who loved him. A successful man, with marvelous stories to tell. Late that night, by the light of a warm stone hearth, with a crowd of people gathered around, Adam told the story of a beautiful faerie girl he met in the forest. How he fell in love with her, how she saved him, and how she disappeared. Children's eyes lit up and mouths hung open. Others yawned and fell asleep. Old men and women marveled to hear the tale. They ran their eyes along his scars and accepted it for truth.

And it became one of their legends.

Finis.

On October 11, 2005 I killed myself. That was about right – Oct. 11. Two years after I met Nathalie. October 11 was a good day, when I killed myself.

I went out with my friends that night, I think. Good people, my friends. Pretty good people. We went out that night and drank some drinks. Wandered to a party that somebody knew of.

Maybe I danced a little and everyone just stared at me. It's a little fuzzy now. Maybe I just had too much energy. That's how it always was with me – too little energy, and then too much.

How can people not embrace the physical? I mean – don't you wonder about it sometimes? Most people are so dead. But me too, but, but then the moment comes and you come alive – isn't it? But most people just stay dead.

Why? Don't you wonder?

They look at you. Scornfully. Why? Dead inside. Or maybe there's something wrong with you – or them. It doesn't matter does it. They still stare at you, and look down.

You always go home all alone. I mean me. Probably not you. And you hate being alone.

I mean me. Probably you too.

Anyway, no point to cry about it. Better to kill yourself – that's what I did.

October 11, 2005. Two years after I met Nathalie. Not because of her, you know, just because.

Were you ever a human being? I mean, physical and visceral. Radiating physical – and emotional.

Do you know what I mean?

Were you an affectionate person, alive inside? We all sometimes fall on the right side of alive. Sometimes we fall on the wrong.

So anyway...

Do you know what I'm talking about? When you lay in bed at night and every inch of your body aches. On the surface, your skin, and deep inside of you. That profound, abiding pain. That comes from never being touched.

Most of us feel it. Some of us feel it too much.

That comes from never being touched. It's why old people want to die, you know. Don't you? Isn't it? Must be, you know.

It's after the first decade that it starts to get to you. That first decade, it seems like no big deal. Doesn't it.

You're all rebellious. Like, I don't need anything from anybody! Like, I stand apart and above. I don't need friends! Much less lovers. I am complete, just in and of myself. 'There are hermit souls that live withdrawn in a fellowless firmament.'

But then the aching starts. In your muscles, in your bones. Your skin starts to tingle, doesn't it. Where someone was supposed to touch it.

But never did.

So you do the usual thing. Prostitution, maybe. Or give some girl you hate a wedding ring. And maybe you love her, because you needed her. She's pretty much the same.

Well, that's what you do.

Instead of that, I decided to kill myself. On October 11, 2005. I expect you didn't hear about it. Nobody cared that I had died. Or maybe they did. I put it out of my mind.

Had to, to get the job done.

It's pretty simple what happens, see. First you see it coming. Somewhere there on the far horizon. A faint tickle in your forward memory. You probably swear an oath. You probably promise not to kill yourself. Ever. Under any circumstance.

After a while it doesn't mean so much.

But you probably found out you believe in God. And suicides go to hell, or some such thing. Did you ever think about how bad hell must be? Think about the worst thing that men could do to you. Now think about the worst thing that God could do to you.

After a while you really don't care. God broke the fucking deal, didn't he? Wasn't there a deal? And sooner or later you realized that He just doesn't give a shit. Prayed for forgiveness as soon as you thought it. Didn't you. But you chose not to accept life in this world. No thanks, I mean. Isn't that what you said? Or did you say, "I reject this world and everything in it!" Then thought of your family and felt like shit. Then wanted to kill yourself again.

At some point you get over the God thing. [God forgive me.]

So then all you have left is your family that you love. If you're lucky you have them. And that's what holds your hand.

You start to resent them, isn't that funny? They stand in the way of you killing yourself. Those fuckers. Not like they really need you. Not like losing you would be a big loss in their life. They just think it would. And they'll hold you to it.

Your family loves you. It would crush them if you killed yourself. Or even if you just lied and died. You can't do it, they won't let you.

Eventually, you forget about them. They just don't figure into the calculation. It's all a haze, and it doesn't make sense. Or makes the only sense.

The calculation goes like this: I want to kill myself. It seems right that I should kill myself. It is appropriate for me to kill myself. I want to die. It would be so nice to die at my own hand. I can kill myself. I can make it stop. When you think about it, it's the only reasonable thing to do. It just feels right. More right than anything. Like maybe this is what I was supposed to do all along. It's what I have to do. Die.

On October 11, I killed myself. I thought about jumping off of my balcony, but I just laid down in the bathtub and cut my veins open. All of them I could. It's more painful that way, that's why. Seemed like I deserved it.

I left a note on the table. I think maybe I scribbled a poem. It was garbled, nobody could read it. I left a note, though. Handwriting, the personal touch.

> Please forgive me. There was nothing anyone
> could have done to help. I don't have any
> secrets or anything like that. I just can't live in
> this world anymore. So tired. Please pray for
> my soul.
>
> Love you all very much.
> Justin